The British author, Joey Marcelle was born in 1988 and raised in Manchester, England. *Nothing Is as It Seems* is the first of what hopes to be a series of books. With a strong passion for creativity, Joey Marcelle works within the entertainment industry. The book was created from her passion and love of reading thrillers. *Nothing Is as It Seems* is an action-fuelled plot that is thought-provoking, gripping, full of suspense and encompasses a variety of themes.

Dedicated to my beautiful mum.
May you always shine and guide over us all.

x

Joey Marcelle

NOTHING IS AS IT SEEMS

A Story About Love, Loss and Obsession

AUSTIN MACAULEY PUBLISHERS™
LONDON • CAMBRIDGE • NEW YORK • SHARJAH

Copyright © Joey Marcelle 2023

The right of Joey Marcelle to be identified as author of this work has been asserted by the author in accordance with sections 77 and 78 of the Copyright, Designs and Patents Act 1988.

All rights reserved. No part of this publication may be reproduced, stored in a retrieval system, or transmitted in any form or by any means, electronic, mechanical, photocopying, recording, or otherwise, without the prior permission of the publishers.

Any person who commits any unauthorised act in relation to this publication may be liable to criminal prosecution and civil claims for damages.

This is a work of fiction. Names, characters, businesses, places, events, locales, and incidents are either the products of the author's imagination or used in a fictitious manner. Any resemblance to actual persons, living or dead, or actual events is purely coincidental.

A CIP catalogue record for this title is available from the British Library.

ISBN 9781035809219 (Paperback)
ISBN 9781035809226 (ePub e-book)

www.austinmacauley.com

First Published 2023
Austin Macauley Publishers Ltd®
1 Canada Square
Canary Wharf
London
E14 5AA

Big thanks to my dad, Ken, for believing in the book and helping in the editing process.

To Ben for being the most loving and supportive partner.

To my sister Nat, family, and friends, thank you for supporting me, always.

Thanks to Austin Macauley for taking a chance on an unknown author.

Chapter 1

The Johnsons look like a picture, perfect family. Sam and Francesca Johnson met nine years ago when they were set up on a double date. When they first met, Francesca had just relocated from her hometown, Milan, Italy to London to fulfil her dream of being a retail buyer at a fashion house in the UK.

The evening had not gone to plan, they seemed to disagree on almost everything, but there was an underlying attraction which intrigued Sam. After a while, he felt the pressure to settle down with a good woman in the hope that it would stop him steering off onto the wrong path.

From the outside, the Johnsons seem to be full of laughter and unconditional love, but the reality is very different. Under the bright, gleaming, idyllic façade, there is a darkness that lies within a hidden past.

Sam Johnson recently accepted a new job in York, so without hesitation Francesca and their children, seven-year-old Nico and five-year-old, Bella packed up their lives and left everything behind. His new job at New Dawn Architects may not have been the promotion he thought he deserved but moving 210 miles north, out of London, creates the much-needed distance from his troubles and to what he hopes and naively believes will be a quieter future, a future where the family can start to create new memories. For the first time in what feels like forever, he breathes deeply and admires his wife.

'This will be an adventure. An exciting new start for us all!' Sam says, glancing in the rear-view mirror at Nico and Bella who are staring excitedly out of the window, watching the pale stone detached houses pass them by.

'We are here, kids,' Sam eagerly says. Their grey Audi 4×4 turns down the drive of their new home. Their home looks like a picture in a magazine, a beautiful semi-detached Victorian house with bay windows, pale green windowsills, and Venetian shutters.

'The house is even more beautiful than the photo,' Francesca says, eyes fixed, gazing up at the house, as she opens the car door

'It is, just wait until you see inside. I have a feeling that we are going to be very happy here,' Sam replies as he saunters confidently around the car. He draws his wife in closely and kisses her affectionately.

The kids charge towards the large oak front door, Sam follows and opens the door to reveal a large, hallway with its original dark, parquet flooring and tall ceilings, typical characteristics of a late nineteenth century Victorian home. Even though the house is dusty and empty, Sam feels more at ease than in their previous house, 'Come on, kids, let's look around. We need to decide who gets which bedroom.' The kids scream with anticipation and run upstairs.

Sam watches his children, taking pleasure in seeing their excitement and joy. It makes him reflect on his own childhood which was a stark contrast. His life growing up in Surrey, London, was privileged yet complicated. His parents focused their attention on building a successful business. Father, Colin Johnson, made a name for himself in textiles, importing fabrics from the Far East, working with local British factories to create beautiful homeware furnishings including unique and expensive rugs, throws and blankets. After 30 years in business, they continue to supply some of the biggest retailers.

His father had always been ruthless in character and when it came to making money. His mother Ava handles the distribution network and retail accounts. Negotiating daily with suppliers has created a fierce businesswoman, one to be feared.

Colin and Ava were absent for a significant part of Sam and his brother, Noah's childhood, prioritising work and travelling abroad on business trips. This distance created little connection between the family and Sam suffered greatly from his parent's absence and lack of emotional support that he has unconsciously developed the habit of attention seeking. Craving the need to be seen and heard. He resents his parents for the dark characteristics he knows he possesses in his personality, a complex mix of insecurity, obsessive traits and the need to seek control within his environment.

Francesca interrupts Sam's spiralling negative thinking with her shouting from their newly modernised kitchen, 'The estate agent have sent a welcome package. That is so kind of them,' Francesca says as she picks up the bottle of champagne and chocolates that lie on the island in the centre of the kitchen.

Sam walks into the kitchen but does not acknowledge or even look at Francesca. He leans on the worktop, looking outwards to their garden, feeling more at ease, thinking of the path that has led him here, to this house, to a city where nobody knows him.

For years, Sam has been trying to escape his past, something which has haunted him. He is worried that, one day, he may be confronted with the repercussions of his previous actions and particularly one event that he isn't proud of. He lives with a heavy, dominating feeling that the truth may come to light, unable to escape, it casts a shadow over him.

As Sam makes his way to work on Monday morning, he leaves the house early to explore the city centre walking on the cobbled streets through York, taking in the surrounding beauty, history and the architecture. Mentally preparing as he approaches his new office, aware of his heart racing, beating fast. Adrenalin starts to shoot through his body, his senses heightening with every step; any attempt at staying calm and composed begins to fade and is replaced by strong thoughts and feelings of apprehension.

Whilst charming at times, Sam's is always concerned and nervous when meeting new people.

He arrives at the office, a plaque for New Dawn Architects is displayed on a terraced building. Even his 6ft stature and athletic frame cannot hide his insecurities and suspicious nature. His big, strong fingers push firmly down on the buzzer. 'Hi, it's Sam Johnson; I am here for my first day.'

'Welcome, Sam, we have been expecting you, come on in.'

Chapter 2

It has been ten months since Lily left her old life in London behind to travel, eventually settling in Australia, even if only for a while. 30-year-old Lily had planned her travels in a coffee shop in Clapham Junction, London, as she drank overpriced, pretentious, bitter coffee. She sat there and noticed the strangers racing by. Men in suits talking loudly on the phone and women smartly dressed, their perfectly styled hair flowing in the wind. They strutted by with a purpose to what Lily imagined were high flying, successful jobs somewhere in the city. Gazing at the businesspeople walking past, she thought growing up that she would be just like them, a successful journalist, happy in life, feeling stable and secure in a job. She wondered, *What was their story? How would they deal with adversity? Would they have travelled down a different path if they were dealt with the same obstacles?*

Lily would never know the answer to these questions. All she does know is that her own life had faced a degree of adversity which led her down a dark, lonely, and isolated path.

She knew for a long time that she needed to escape her life and create a new path for herself. A path without complication and one which, she very much hoped would lead to self-contentment and happiness. She trawled through travel guides acquired from various local travel agents, scrutinising every detail, deciding where to visit? How long for? Would her money stretch to all those destinations? She had sounded out those friends who had travelled to get their experience and suggestions before she finalised a well-defined route and booked flights to Europe, Thailand, New Zealand, and finally Australia. The trip sounded perfect, just what she needed, the idea of travelling the world gave her a sense of purpose. She may not have a high-flying job, but her travel adventure would be her own success story.

For some time, Lily had this overriding fear that she was getting left behind in life, seeing everyone else around her sprint forward, achieving, while she stood still as time passed by. She desperately needed to feel connected to something bigger, so she packed up and left home with her life savings, mosquito repellent and backpack in tow. When she left London, she believed, hoped that travelling would give her a sense of purpose and whilst at first it did, as the months unfolded, she began to feel more lost, more disconnected from herself and her beliefs about what truly mattered.

Lily hadn't always felt this need to escape, her childhood was as perfect as any childhood could be; a loving family where Saturday mornings were filled with baking cookies and listening to music. There was always an abundance of love and laughter. Lily and her brother Peter felt protected and cared for. Even with all the after-school activities of sports and piano lessons, there was always one parent there to encourage and cheer them on. As a child Lily was fearless, believing that she could do, achieve anything.

Being fearless was a trait instilled in her by her parents, Jean and Bill. Their unconditional love radiated throughout the house, an ideal vision for what a loving partnership should be like, supportive, caring and always fun, even if they did have opposing views at times. Witnessing this shaped Lily how she saw and behaved in her own relationships. In her formative years, Lily found it easy to form deep, meaningful connections, firstly with her friends and then in relationships. She never feared that one day a loved one may leave or even abandon her.

The light midday sun streams into the room slowly awakening Lily, who is still wearing last night's clothes, denim shorts and a washed-out t-shirt. Her wrists are filled with bangles and wristbands from concerts she has attended which jingle as she stretches, her head and body feeling heavy and clouded. Lily forces herself out of bed. She is living in a small communal house near Victoria Park, around a 20 minutes' walk from Darling Harbour, Sydney, with two housemates, Oliver and Sara who are making lunch and chatting loudly downstairs. There isn't much quiet time in the house or in the life she has created but Lily welcomes this as a nice distraction from the noise constantly playing on a loop in her head. Oliver, Sara, and Lily had been travelling solo before their lives crossed and they all decided to settle in Sydney to work and save money, before continuing with their adventures. Despite her inner turmoil and dread, the house has a great, positive energy, a sense of familiarity and safety.

Oliver is a confident and charming 25-year-old from Leeds whilst Sara, from Spain, displays an ease and kindness, no matter the situation, a characteristic Lily is in awe of.

Lily staggers down the stairs, her unkept hair falling untidily over her face, exposing the residue of last night's makeup that has smudged across her tired face.

Oliver looks up at Lily as she arrives into the room, 'Morning, sorry, afternoon Lils,' he says smirking as he sips his tea.

Lily rubs her eyes, as if to further wake herself up, 'Morning.'

'Good night then?' He says as he notices she is still wearing the same clothes from the night before.

'Something like that.'

'I am making some lunch if you fancy?'

Lily looks down at her watch. 'That's kind but I best jump into the shower before I head off to work.'

Oliver looks on compassionately, 'You need to eat something. I will fix you up a sandwich, you can eat it on the way to work.'

'Thank you. That would be great' Lily is appreciative of someone looking after her.

She is working as a bartender in a downtown dive bar, The Tap Club, a favourite for both locals and travellers. She doesn't know how long she will be working there for, just long enough to save up to travel and explore the East Coast – wanting to pass through Byron Bay, Fraser Island, and ending in Cairns. Even though thousands of miles from England, the bar feels like home. Lily is intrigued by people, their character and why people are the way they are. Serving and making them drinks is a great way for her to engage with total strangers. She loves asking them questions, intrigued about their life and character, finding out why they left their hometown? Were they running away from something and if so, what was it? Would they tell her? Lily takes this information and tries to piece together a picture of what their life is like. It is in these conversations with total strangers that she has time to reflect on her own life, the friends and family that she has left behind. But Lily is never forthcoming about herself, not wanting to give people too much insight into her own life; it is just too painful, not wanting to shine a light on her fears. She knows how dangerous it is to keep her feelings and thoughts locked up, hidden, so recently she took the brave step to seek therapy, hoping it may help to unravel, untangle, herself. For many years Lily had looked after those around her, whilst neglecting her own needs so therapy was a terrifying leap, but one she knew she had to take. Fearing that if she doesn't work on herself, she will continue to live a lie. A life which is numbed by alcohol, an unhelpful tool used to escape the trauma and demons of her past. Demons that constantly appear in her shadows, haunting her.

Chapter 3

Sam walks into a large open plan office that is filled with people talking over their desks. They all look up as he enters. A tall man, wearing round glasses, a tweed jacket and light shirt walks towards him. He reaches out to Sam and greets him with a firm handshake.

Robert, the Managing Partner greets him, 'Hi Sam, I'm Robert. Welcome to New Dawn Architects. We are delighted you have decided to join us.'

'Thanks, I look forward to being part of the team,' Sam says as he shakes his hand firmly.

'Why don't you come into my office? We can have a chat and then I will introduce you to the rest of the folk.'

Robert heads into his office with Sam following, they both take a seat. Robert continues, 'Moving from London to York will be a big change, I hope you are ready for it.'

'I am glad to have left London; it can sometimes be…'

There is a long pause, Sam looks down to his hands that are resting on his knees.

'Overwhelming?' Robert asked.

'Yes, something like that.' Sam looks up to meet Robert's eyes again.

'Where have you moved too?' Robert asked, inquisitively.

'Park Avenue, about a 20 minutes' walk from here.'

'It is lovely around there! Paul Adams told me a lot about you, he was very impressed with you in the interview and mentioned your portfolio of work in London. The scheme you did near Waterloo was, spectacular.'

'Thanks, I admit I do slightly obsess and fixate over details but that, to me, is where the beauty of a project lies. I believe the small details are what make the complete architectural design standout.'

Robert enthusiastically nods his head, 'I couldn't agree more. What are you most looking forward to about being in York then?'

'I don't know,'—there is another pause before Sam continues,—'I suppose, starting again, a new challenge.'

'Good, well then, let me introduce you to the team,' Robert drinks his coffee and places it on the table, then walks out of his office.

'Everyone, meet Sam Johnson.' Robert projects his voice across the room, grabbing everyone's attention, 'Sam has come from Atlas Architects in London. If you aren't familiar with his work, it's impressive and well worth getting to know. I'm sure you will all make him feel very welcome.'

Sam settles into his new desk space located by big industrial, black paned windows, overlooking the cobbled streets. One by one his new colleagues walk over to introduce themselves, and with each new introduction, Sam feels himself becoming more and more agitated, despite the beaming smiles around him. He needs control but in this new, unfamiliar environment with people that he doesn't know all asking him personal questions, he begins to feel suffocated. To cover his frustration, Sam starts to overcompensate by leading the conversation, asking his colleagues questions, turning the attention onto them. Feeling more in control his fake smile grows bigger, he pumps his chest out, the false laughter between him and his new colleagues becoming louder.

He creates an abrupt ending to the awkward introductions stating directly, 'Nice to meet you all but I must get on, otherwise Robert will be wondering why he employed me.' He then focuses his attention on the firm's portfolio, spending the remainder of the day looking, and analysing previous work. Sam finds the company has a different creative style and flair from a lot of the developments and projects he was previously involved in, even so he was ready to take on the challenge.

At the day's end, Robert strolls over to him. 'Hope you had a good day, meeting the team and getting to know how we do things around here. It seems you have met everyone, everyone except Olivia and Dan who are on a site visit and pitching for a new project in Leeds. I always prefer to send two people to a pitch. I feel that the dynamic of two architects brings two different visions to the task. Anyway, I will arrange a welcome dinner for you later this week.'

'That sounds great,' Sam replies with little enthusiasm. A welcome dinner is the last place Sam wants to be as he doesn't enjoy sitting around making small talk, knowing his new colleagues will be eager to get to know him, asking questions about his old life in London.

A life that he is keen to forget!

Chapter 4

Every Wednesday feels the same, an overriding crashing wave of intolerable, uncomfortable feelings. Lily's body is tense, there is a great sensation of tightness across her chest, butterflies racing around her stomach. Shifting out of bed, she creeps over to the bedroom door, an attempt to not disturb Charlie, her latest love interest. His dark olive skin and green eyes initially attracted Lily when they met at, The Tap Bar, a month ago. When they met, Lily was serving drinks to Charlie and his mate from work, another expat.

In the most intriguing, genuine manner, he said, 'Alright, love,'

Lily was immediately charmed by his confidence and tried to pinpoint his accent.

'What can I get you?' Lily replied quietly, in her most seductive tone, an attempt to appear confident and relaxed.

Oblivious to the reaction he was having on her, he just responds with, 'Two Fosters, please,' before returning to his conversation.

Without a word she places the beers in front of them as they sit on the bar stools.

Lily didn't know anything about this stranger, but his energy had sparked her interest. On her walk home that night, she created stories in her mind, fantasy conversations about how they talked for hours. How he had asked her interesting questions. In her mind, Lily had become more open and vulnerable as they continued to chat. The prospect of Lily forming a deeper connection with a partner is something she very much craved and needed. But Lily has been very closed off, struggling to trust many men outside her family and therapist, Mr. Lint, but it seemed as if there was something different about Charlie.

After their brief encounter, she would occasionally think about this mystery man. She had almost put him out of her mind until one day last month when he wandered in alone, back into the bar.

Being his bartender gave her a false sense of confidence, a reason to talk to him, wanting to know everything about this stranger. This was her moment to pluck up the courage and say something apart from taking his drinks order. As he sat drinking whisky on the rocks they began to talk about their lives, how Charlie was from Manchester, England and missed his family back home and the life events that had led him wanting to travel to Australia, if even for a moment. As they talked, Lily started to feel a connection, an authenticity to their conversation; she couldn't let Charlie leave without getting his number.

Over the last month their relationship has developed, a combination of great sex, interesting conversation and laughter. Meeting Charlie has given Lily a feeling that, at last, she has found someone she can have a meaningful relationship with, and being so far from home Lily welcomes this connection.

Lily turns the bedroom door handle, she looks back to see Charlie peacefully asleep. She smiles to herself, instantly feeling calmer. She focuses on her usual morning routine before therapy, the always panicked rush around the house.

There are a thousand places Lily would rather be then at therapy, tucked up in bed with Charlie is definitely one of them. Instead, she makes her way towards the bus stop and heads into the city. Taking her headphones out of her handbag, she plays the latest John Mayer album, the soft melodies and his guitar solos soothe her through the speakers. Suddenly, a flashback of her family singing and dancing around the kitchen table vividly enters her mind; images powerful, heart-breaking and moving all at the same time as if she is watching a movie in front of her. The star of the show, her mum Jean is dancing, gliding, around the kitchen, her feet moving to every beat, the long skirt swirling as she dances. When she dances, she would lose all inhibitions, her muscles loose and relaxed, totally present in the moment. In this vision, Lily and Peter would look on adoringly at their mum, amazed at her confidence and carefree nature. Jean was one of those rare, free spirits who could easily get lost in a good song, a great book and would feel content when spending time with her family. Her vibrant, kind, and caring nature connected easily to people around her.

The piercing sound of a car horn jolts Lily back to reality. Lily never imagined she would need to seek therapy whilst travelling but deep down she knows it is the right step to take. She feels undeniably guilty of some of her actions and needs to find a way to leave the past behind, accept who she is and move forward with a greater level of self-confidence.

She found Mr. Lint on the Arcap register, the Register for Australian Counsellors and Psychotherapists. His list of degrees, qualifications and work history sat next to a small photograph on the website. The photo showed a man wearing thick, orange rimmed glasses, dark blonde hair, and blue eyes. His face looked warm and inviting. Going with her gut feeling Lily had booked her first session five weeks ago without hesitation, even if he did charge 150 dollars an hour for his service. This is the one luxury Lily gives herself, more of a necessity than a luxury she believes.

Over the five weeks a rapport and level of trust has grown. Lily enjoys his slight nerdiness and quirky mannerisms. She wondered if he had a family, kids and what were they like? Was he as calm with them as he was with Lily? How did he resolve disagreements with his wife?

Lily takes the elevator to the fifth floor and nervously enters the large reception, apprehensive as she knows she is there to expose more of her true self and the parts she keeps hidden. After a few minutes, the receptionist calls her name. Lily stands up, looks over at the receptionist as she continues, 'Mr. Lint will see you now.'

She enters the room, it is warmly lit, decorated with earthy colours and several Japanese artworks hang on the walls. There is a big light grey sofa and an armchair opposite. Lavender and sandalwood tones circulate the room, creating an energy of calm relaxation.

Lily flings her denim fringed jacket and heavy handbag onto the sofa, breathing heavily before falling back to face Mr. Lint who is sat cross legged in his usual armchair. He wears a light knitted sweatshirt, corduroy beige trousers, multicolour socks and brown loafers. His vibrant socks are a contrast to his muted outfit. Deep down Lily feels grateful for the one-hour sessions even when feeling dread knowing that she is about to delve deeper into her core emotions.

'So, Lily, how has your week been?'

'Better, I suppose.'

'That's good, better in what way?' Mr. Lint presses.

'Well, I have been creating space to meditate.'

'I am glad to hear that, it is so important. Do you feel like you can embed meditation as a habit into your daily ritual?'

'Well, I hope so, I do see the benefits.' A small smile cracks onto Lily's face.

'What about other habits? Are you getting enough sleep?'

'That is difficult. I am working so many night shifts so I can save up and travel, hopefully in a couple of months' time.'

'I understand that but how is the quality of your sleep?'

There is a long pause, silence vibrating throughout the stillness in the room.

'OK, I suppose,' Lily stutters.

Mr Lint responds after a slight pause, 'Just, OK?'

Lily responds slowly, 'I am having…dreams, the same recurring dreams.'

Mr. Lint notices a shift in Lily so presses delicately, 'What happens in these dreams?'

'They are more like nightmares, reliving a time I would rather forget.' A look of sadness and despondency crosses her face.

'Are you OK if we dig a little deeper and look at that in more detail?' Mr Lint asks compassionately.

Lily shakes her head, her body language now shifting into an almost child-like state, crouching over, as she places her head in her hands, a sense of despair leaking from every pore.

'This is your time, Lily. Why don't we come back to this when you are ready?'

There is no response.

'Only if you want too?' Mr. Lint starts to guide the conversation in a different direction. 'How is your relationship with Charlie then?'

Lily moves her hands away from protecting her face, smiles slightly and falls back into the sofa; this question is a lot easier to answer, even though a little complicated.

Chapter 5

Sam wanders back home, exhausted from the mundane small talk, glad the first day is over. As he heads home, he doesn't want to face Francesca and the kids, not just yet, with what he believes will be a barrage of questions. How was your first day? What is the team like? Have they put you onto a scheme? The thought of this interrogation immediately irritates him. As he continues down the street past York's famous Tea Shop, he looks inside to see people playing happy families eating scones with cream and jam, kids laughing, parents looking lovingly at each other and at their children. Sam scowls at this picture of perfect bliss and finds himself marching aggressively into the nearest pub.

He orders a single malt whisky and takes a seat in the corner of the room. His large, bear-like hands lift the short glass, he swallows the smoky liquid in one large mouthful. He doesn't wait to taste the smokiness of the liquid; he just needs it to take effect and take the edge of the day. He looks around the pub; no one knows who he is, his reputation, or anything about his life. The reminder of being anonymous, just another stranger relaxes him further into his seat. Away from London, his childhood home of Surrey and then Hampstead Village, where the family lived for many years, he is appreciative of his anonymity in York. He looks around the pub again, investigating his surroundings. He doesn't sense any small whispers or strange glances being directed towards him. Feeling more comfortable, he orders another whisky. Sam finally looks down at his watch and notices the time is nearly 7:45 pm so pulls his phone out of his pocket. Four missed calls from Francesca and a text sent an hour ago that reads, 'How was your first day, are you coming home for dinner?'

Sam has a warm sensation running around his body from the whisky. Without responding, he stands up and now in a more casual state of mind heads out of the pub door towards home. On arrival, Nico and Bella race into the hall at the sound of him putting his keys into the front door.

'Hi, Daddy, how was your day?' Nico says.

'Are you the boss there?' Bella excitedly enquires.

'It was great, thanks, kids.'

The homely smell of his wife's Italian cooking fills the air. Sam sweeps Bella up into his arms and wanders into the kitchen. Utensils, garlic cloves, the pasta maker lie across the kitchen island. Their new oak dining table was set for two, candles lit with jazz playing quietly in the background. Sam realises Francesca has tried to create a special dinner. When Francesca cooks, she cooks the Italian way with a full heart, a way of showing her love and affection. He walks over to Francesca, who is standing at the hob and as she ladles the ragu into bowls, he hugs her from behind and whispers, 'Cesca, dinner smells great.'

They sit down for a civilised dinner. Sam tries to not punish Francesca for asking what would be considered normal questions about his day, his new colleagues.

Francesca looks empathetically at Sam, 'I know you haven't been yourself recently, I am just checking in, I want you to really enjoy your new job.'

'Thanks, babe,' Sam responds, giving a small smile. He then continues, softening his manner, 'Come on, I will finish washing up, you run yourself a nice bath, I will be up soon.'

He watches the football highlights on his phone as he washes the dishes and has another small whisky. The kids are in bed, the house is quiet. He stumbles upstairs and sees Francesca seductively wearing her black, lace nightdress; the spaghetti straps hanging loosely over her bronzed shoulders. The room is dimly lit, moody. Their eyes met across the bedroom. Time stops. Sam walks confidently over to Cesca. As he kisses her neck, her nightdress straps fall further down seductively exposing her breasts. Sam's lips gently caress her skin, his hands confident with every move. They run over her stomach, down her legs and between her thighs. He slowly pulls down her underwear. Their bodies move together, movements in sync, as their breathing quickens. Sam sits up and takes off his top and pulls his trousers down. Cesca looks on as he towers above her, her body feeling warmer and tense. Getting into bed, they fall into each other naturally; the way they have done countless times before. Francesca lets him know that she wants him, a statement that gives Sam a thrill, exciting him further. He loves more than anything the feeling of power that comes from Francesca needing him.

Over the next couple of days, the Johnson family adapt to their new way of live in York, settling into their house which is beginning to look more like a home. Nico and Bella have started at their new school; each night they relay stories about teachers, the classes, and the friends they are starting to make.

Sam and Cesca take this information overload as enthusiasm, feeling at ease knowing their children are happy and doing well to readjust.

Over the coming days, Sam becomes more comfortable with his colleagues, feeling slightly less awkward. Before he knows it, it is Thursday, awaiting his welcome dinner at the local Italian restaurant, Gabrielle's, a quaint, intimate restaurant renowned for its welcoming staff and authentic Italian food. Candles lie on the green, red and white tablecloths. The fragrant smell of tomatoes and garlic excite the senses as soon as you enter. Sam scans the room and wonders if their reservation of ten people will overwhelm this tiny, family run restaurant.

He arrives half an hour late, using the excuse of finishing work in the office. He sits himself in the vacant seat next to Robert, not looking around to see who else is at the table.

Sam apologises to Robert, 'Sorry I am late, I had my head in the requirements of the Clifton scheme.'

'Don't worry, all good,' replies Robert.

Sam analyses the menu. 'What's good to eat here then?'

'The Chicken Milanese is a crowd pleaser.'

'OK, that's it, I'll have that.' He says shutting the menu quickly and taking a large gulp of his Amarone, that has been poured into a large glass, in front of him.

After a while his agitation fades as he settles into the evening, finally looking around to notice the rest of his colleagues at the table.

Suddenly, he sees an unknown face at the other end of the table, a woman engaging in conversation with the person sat opposite to her. He sits there, transfixed, taking in her every detail. Analysing her long, dark curly hair and light hazel eyes that seem to glisten and smile as she speaks. Sam doesn't know who she is or why she is there but instantly feels drawn to her, desperately wanting to know more. Looking at her, admiring her from a far, for a moment he forgets that there are other people in the room.

As the evening rolls on and the team talk business, Sam laughs falsely to the witty jokes being made, all the while obsessing, wondering when he will be introduced to this mysterious woman. Eventually Robert waves over the people at the end of the table to come over and join them. Sam appears to be uninterested, secretly counting down the moments before he will finally be introduced to this woman. After a re-arrangement of the chairs, she is sitting on the other side of the table, in his direct eye line. She is even more striking up close, impossible as that was, he thinks. Sam fixates over her characteristics, absorbing her features, watching as her freckles dance beautifully across her nose and cheeks. His hands start to feel hot and sweaty; he begins to fidget in his chair, trying to get comfortable. At least the Amarone has given a false sense of Dutch courage.

Their eyes now firmly fixed on each other, electricity sparking between them.

Robert interrupts this unspoken moment. 'I've just realised you two haven't been introduced, sorry about that. Sam, I mentioned that Olivia has been working in Leeds pitching for a new development so has not been in the office.' Sitting in complete stillness Olivia tilts her head slightly to the side, eyes still firmly fixed on Sam. Robert is oblivious to their glances and continues to talk with a large glass of red wine in hand, 'Olivia Bloom is one of our top architects. We are lucky to have her as part of the team. She is a rising star and has already been recognised by the RIBA. As well as being nominated last year for her design of the new Dawson office development.'

'Well done, what an achievement,' Sam responds enthusiastically.

'Thanks, but I didn't win,' Olivia replies.

Sam bites his lip and says, 'Still, the nomination is very commendable.'

Olivia's eyes widen slightly.

Robert continues, 'Yes very. Olivia, we are lucky to welcome Sam as part of the team. He has recently joined us from Atlas Architects.'

'Didn't Atlas win the office scheme in the Embankment, London?' Olivia inquisitively asks, 'Were you involved in that?'

'Yes, actually I led that project.' As he says these words, Sam becomes more confident, realising his success and portfolio of work in London is something to be proud of and a good basis for a conversation.

Olivia is intrigued as to why someone would relocate and leave behind such noteworthy projects, 'It must be a big change leaving the team in London and coming here to York, so what you made you want to move?'

'A number of factors really, a change is sometimes needed, I suppose,' Sam answers.

Robert looks at his watch and then over at Sam. 'Right, now I think you know everyone here, I am going to leave as I have a new client meeting tomorrow and need to be on top form. Any more Amarone, I will struggle.' He puts his corporate Amex on the bill in front of him.

'Have a good night, everyone.' He says as he picks up the bill and heads over to the bar to pay.

Sam and Olivia are too involved in their own conversation to notice that most of their other colleagues have also left.

'So, Olivia, what do you like to do when you are not working?'

'Not much really. I suppose I live a quiet life, like to work out, Yoga, see friends.'

He can't control himself. He must know more. 'Quiet life? I take it you don't have kids then?' Does she have kids? A partner? How much digging can he do without it being obvious?

'Kids, no!' Her eyes communicate signs of deep regret and sadness. 'Children were always part of my plan but for one reason or another, it just wasn't meant to be.' Olivia gazes down in deep thought, she finally responds, 'How about you. Do you have children?'

Sam thinks intently about how to answer, he is torn. One part of him is encouraging him to be truthful, to talk about his children and wife, the other side, fiercely pulling him back, not wanting to tell her he is married. He knows his interest in this beautiful woman is wrong. He can't help it, he is mesmerised. The tension and energy between them are almost tangible, the atmosphere around them, heavy. Sam is amazed at how easily their conversation flows.

With keen interest and pleasure, he notices her every detail, the small glances, the way she slowly looks up and down, in a flirtatious manner. The way she touches her face, the small flicks of her hair. Guiltily, he knows he is feeling something and wonders if Olivia also feels the chemistry.

Sam finally says, 'I have two children. Nico is seven and Bella is five.'

'Oh, that's lovely.' Olivia's tone contains a slight air of disappointment; her response doesn't seem to Sam to be totally genuine.

Engrossed in their conversation, Olivia notices the recent absence of her colleagues. They are now all alone with just the bare candle softening the charged air between them.

'It's getting late, well it is lovely to meet you…Sam.' Olivia looks out of the corner of her eye and stands up to put her beige woollen jacket on, tying the jacket around her waist to cover her black dress. Sam notices her curvy shape and slender bare legs which are now fully in view and looks on in awe.

'Good night, Olivia.' Sam continues to drink, alone in the restaurant for a while longer. A mixture of feelings and thoughts fill his mind. There are so many questions he must ask Olivia, so much more he wants, needs to discover.

Sam leaves the restaurant bewildered; obsessing, fantasizing over a woman that he doesn't even know. Will he be willing to take the risk and get to know this woman? His heart and head in total conflict.

Chapter 6

Looking out of the window, Lily is in a daydream as she studies the cloud formations.

'So…how is Charlie then?' Mr. Lint repeats the question.

'He is great, we seem to be growing closer.'

Mr. Lint allows Lily to control and steer the conversation.

Lily is acutely aware of the silence so fills it with words. 'We are getting closer. It has been over a month now. I just don't want my own concerns to tarnish the relationship. Sometimes I can't stop over-analysing, worrying, and agonising over questions. Will he leave me? Am I good enough?'

'Does he know you feel like this?'

'No, I am trying to push these feelings down. I know it isn't helpful, we are still at the start of our relationship and getting to know each other. But I still have this unconscious concern that he will see me for who I am and leave.'

'So, what is your perspective of who you think you are then?' Mr. Lint asks delicately, trying to understand the essence of Lily, her identity about who she believes she is.

'At times, I just feel lost and vulnerable. More than anything I have this overwhelming, debilitating fear of abandonment.'

'We touched on this in previous sessions shall we look again at where you feel this vulnerability and feeling of abandonment stems from?'

Lily shuffles anxiously on the couch, struggling to sit still. Conflicting thoughts overwhelm, drown Lily's mind. Finally, Lily cuts through the silence and answers, 'OK.' Lily exhales deeply. 'Where do I start?'

There is another long pause.

'I grew up with great role models of love. Mum and Dad were connected, totally connected, on every level. Of course, there were disagreements like any normal relationship, but they managed to work through the tough times, no matter what. It was unconditional love, you know. Fucking unconditional…' Lily's voice trails off with a raising anger in her tone.

'Seeing this level of love, affected me in the best sort of way. In my teens, I was confident, and carefree. So carefree, just full of life and energy. I hadn't faced any sort of trauma. At the time I hadn't experienced the meaning of loss and heartache. I had no fears, i felt so secure.'

Mr. Lint looks on quietly.

Lily carries on, stomach rising and falling from the enormity of the conversation. 'In my teens, I had no expectation or fear when I was in relationships. I wasn't scared of feeling pain or heartache. I didn't over think anything, it made me a lot more relaxed and easier to be with, I suppose. But as I got older and after various life events happened, I struggled to get back to that carefree version of myself.'

Mr. Lint responds, 'Events, Lily? What events are you referring too?'

'Well…for a start, losing my mum and the pain that caused. I also experienced other things that I would rather forget.' There was a long pause. 'This has all affected me so that now, if I do get close to someone, I am terrified they will leave me.'

'Lily, this is all great. I can see there is a lot here. Are you OK if we start with your mum? What was her name?'

'Mum? Her name was Jean. I was 20 years old when she died. It has been ten years, but the magnitude of the loss has remained, even after all these years. I suppose you never get over such a significant loss. As time passes, you just learn how to deal with it, but I don't always handle my feelings in the best way.'

'That is understandable, you were so young,' Mr. Lint's says compassionately.

'I suppose so.'

'How was the grieving process for you? Did you have the support you needed from people around you, family, friends?'

'My friends and family rallied around me, which is something I will be forever grateful for but there is nothing that can ever prepare you in dealing with losing a parent. It was tough, I hit rock bottom. I felt like I was constantly living in a dark tunnel. I remember there was a time in December when my mum was sick, it was so cold outside and there was no light whatsoever. It felt like a total reflection of how I was feeling on the inside; I was this empty void, unable to see any light or a way through all that darkness.'

'After Mum passed, Dad and brother, Peter became my priority, I felt like it was my job to make sure they were coping. In that, I suppose I did neglect myself. I had intense feelings of pain, anger, sadness, which all boiled up. At the time I didn't know how to cope or direct my energy in a positive way.'

'So, what were your coping strategies?'

'Alcohol. I drank to oblivion. I drank to forget everything, to feel numb. I was tired of feeling so many emotions, I just wanted to feel nothing.'

'Did it help?'

'No,' Lily immediately responded.

'Do you still turn to drinking to cope?'

'I am not going to lie. Yes, sometimes.'

She looks to the ground, a flash of disappointment crosses onto her face, "Well, it's more than just sometimes." Mr. Lint notices the despair, 'We have previously touched on healthy coping strategies, but I think it's important for us to revisit them. You, Lily, have all the tools you need, they are all within you. We need to look at your physical health first, making sure you eat right, keep hydrated and limit, if possible, alcohol consumption.' He continues, 'You are creative and love to read and write. Are there other ways you feel you can channel your energy? I know there is a budding journalist within you, so would highly recommend journaling your feelings, thoughts, when you get into these thinking patterns. Writing down your thoughts daily can be a very helpful and beneficial exercise. This may be difficult at first, but try and persist, it will get easier.'

'Thanks.' Lily smiles, accepting the advice given.

'You also mentioned events that happened in your past that trigger you?'

A deafening silence fills the room. Flashes of a distant memory comes into full focus, bright, vivid pictures bounce through her mind. Lily shakes her head as if to dispel the memory, she is in the depths of a sensory overload.

Lily lets out a long sigh. 'Can we discuss that next week please; I can't do this now?'

Mr. Lint looks at the electronic clock opposite to see that they are nearing the end of their session. 'Of course, we can. Great work today, Lily. I can appreciate its difficult but there is progress here, so be proud of yourself.'

After the sessions, Lily welcomes the feeling after leaving the office, exhausted and emotionally drained, yet reflective. Reflecting on what was said but more importantly what was not said.

Chapter 7

When the family moved to York, Sam had hoped that all the drama would be left back in London, and York would be somewhere he could fly under the radar, stay relatively unknown and start again.

But, as the weeks roll on, the tension between Sam and Olivia increases with every conversation or moment they share, their platonic relationship starting to shift into something different.

Sam walks into the office expecting a normal day only to notice some excitement stirring in a conversation between Olivia and Robert. He watches through the glass office door, seeing them chatting animatedly. Robert notices Sam looking over and walks over to the door, as he opens, he demands, 'Sam, just the man I need, drop your bags and come in here please.'

Sam goes to his desk, puts his laptop bag on the table and walks into Robert's office. 'Morning, how are you?' He tries to ignore Olivia's gaze, instead focusing his full attention on Robert.

'Great, thanks, Sam. I have just been sharing some good news with Olivia. We have been given the opportunity to pitch to the renowned Isla Bourne. You may not know her, but she is an incredibly smart developer at Briggs Property Group. They have a new 70,000 square ft office development and are looking to appoint the right team to take the scheme forward. I have decided to put you two on the task, working together as a team. There is a great energy between you both and with your contrasting but complimentary visions, I think, actually I know, you will develop something magical. How do you feel about that?' Robert takes a quick breath and continues, 'Just to add, the brief has come through with a very short deadline. This needs to be turned around within the next week as the pitch is next Thursday. Are you up for the opportunity?'

'Yes thanks, Robert, this is very exciting. We will do our best to make you proud.' Olivia smiles as she speaks.

Sam does not respond.

'Sam, everything OK with that?' Robert answers, not expecting to have to push for an answer.

'Yes of course, thanks for thinking of us both.'

As they walk out of the office, Sam turns to Olivia and says boldly, 'Well this should be fun; I am looking forward to working with you, Miss Bloom.'

'Likewise. I am excited to understand and see more of your vision come to life,' Olivia responds in a flirtatious manner.

'We don't have much time; shall we make a start this afternoon? I have some time free; we can run through initial ideas?' Sam says to Olivia.

Olivia responds with, 'Let me check my whereabouts!' She pulls out her phone, opening her calendar. 'Yes, that works for me.'

'Great, chat later!'

Sam's intense nature is starting to surface ever since he met Olivia, he has an overriding urge to be closer to her. He knows working alongside her will be the ultimate test for his marriage.

He questions if he can stay faithful, knowing his reserves of self-restraint and control are limited. He does not know how things will develop between them. The not knowing, anticipation of it all is dangerous, but the danger and excitement thrills Sam.

With the short deadline of just over a week to turn around the presentation to Isla Bourne, late nights in the office followed, takeaway boxes trailed over initial sketches and drawings. There were numerous conversations about the design vision, approach, structural issues, likely responses from the planners, as well as the internal functionality of the building. Mutual tired eyes and worn-out faces clearly show across both of their faces. Even with tired eyes, Sam can't help notice the depth and beauty that would glimmer in her eyes in the evening light as they talked for hours.

Before they know it, the day of the presentation arrived.

The introductory meeting with Isla is at her office. Sam and Olivia jump into a taxi and head to the meeting, eventually stopping outside the Briggs office building. Before they walk into reception, Sam lets out a full, deep breath, pumping himself up, ready and focused to give the presentation everything he has got.

Mrs. Bourne greets them in reception, wearing a tweed trouser suit. She carries an air of confidence and respect.

'Lovely to meet you, I am Isla Bourne.'

'Hi there, Isla, I am Sam, and this is Olivia,' he says, confidently reaching out first to shake her hand.

Sam looks back at Olivia; she knows he is going to take the lead. Olivia is eager to see how he will drive the meeting forward and get the result they want.

'I'm sorry but I don't have much time today, I am back-to-back with appointments,' Isla states, pressing the lift button.

Sam reads in between the lines and knows that what Isla is saying is that she is meeting other architects that are all competing to win the scheme. This information fuels Sam's competitive nature and gives him the added incentive to succeed. Sam is a man who wants what he wants, sometimes with no care or consideration for anything or anyone else. A win would be important to show Olivia, his new company that he is up to the job.

As they enter the board room, Sam sets up the presentation, knowing they are short on time, plugging his laptop into the HDMI cable that is connected to a large screen at the end of the boardroom. He confidently stands up, clicking on his laptop, pointing at elements on the screen, talking through details of their design. As Sam presents, Olivia finds moments to add valuable insight and analysis. Together, they work as a team, bouncing off each other, bringing a strong energy to the project. Isla Bourne sits back, silent, still. Her demeanour is making it a challenge for Sam and Olivia to read her reaction. They notice the occasional moments, head nods, small smiles, where she does seem to be fully engaged in the scheme. Towards the end of the presentation, she asks about lead times and delivery until she finally concludes the meeting with, 'Well, Sam, Olivia, that was very unexpected, interesting, I must say! My thanks to both of you. I will be in touch in the next couple of days.'

Sam and Olivia know they have done all they can, they have given it their all. The outcome is now out of their hands.

Leaving the office, Olivia says confidently to Sam, 'Well done. You were great in there.'

'Thanks, so were you!!! How about a celebratory drink?' Sam replies.

'Sounds great, I know a great little spot around the corner.'

Sam smiles, fantasising once again about the possibilities of what he hopes might follow.

Chapter 8

Lily leaves Mr. Lint's office exhausted from the issues uncovered in today's session. She heads home, desperately needing to rest. Her mind needs a break. At the house, Charlie has already left for work. She is glad that she doesn't have to think about a response to Charlie's questioning about the therapy session.

Lily crawls back into bed, fully clothed, resting her head, eyelids heavy. She reflects on her relationship with Charlie, so far there have been no red flags, instead he makes her feel protected and safe.

As she reflects a small smile comes to her face, which immediately turns into a frown as she reminds herself that there is a time limit on their time together. It was always in her plans to leave Sydney and travel the coast. Leaving Sydney means that there is not the added pressure, conversation about the status of their relationship. With no pressure, Lily doesn't need to think too far ahead, instead living in the present, enjoying the time they do have together, however short, or long, that may be.

She drifts off into a light sleep, awaking hours later. Feeling rested, Lily looks forward to the evening ahead. A night out is just what she needs, a welcome distraction from the days therapy session. She needs to disconnect from her spiralling unwanted and unhelpful emotions.

She hears Sara playing music in the kitchen, the base echoing throughout the house, Lily walks down the stairs to join her, ready for their adventure ahead. They pop open a bottle of sparkling wine, Lily puts the words of Mr. Lint aside and takes a long sip from her glass, knowing this will be the first of many drinks to come.

As she gulps, Sara looks over to her and with full empathy asks, 'How was your session with Mr. Lint today?'

Lily absorbs the kindness and concern, grateful for her friendship with Sara, even if she knows that they are at different stages in their life. Sara is so content with herself, relaxed, never overanalysing anything, so when she does drink it is to have fun, whereas Lily lives within the constraints and fears of her own mind, running away from her true feelings.

'Insightful as always, but it is just totally exhausting.'

'Are you seeing the benefits though?'

Lily shifts anxiously, 'Yes, but I just have so much to work through.'

Sara makes a small reassuring smile, 'Don't we all. I can't imagine how scary it must be to go. I am so proud of you for doing so.'

'Being vulnerable with someone else is scary, I think with everything I have been through, it is important.

Sara puts her glass down, giving her full attention to Lily, 'You never really talk about your past. Whenever I ask you skirt around the question. Want to talk about it?'

Lily darts her eye line away from Sara, feeling self-conscious as she responds, 'No, not tonight, let's go to The

Hunt, I need to listen to live music, dance and for us to have some fun!'

'OK, you do know that I am always here whenever you need me.'

'I know that. Thanks, Sara, I really appreciate it.' Lily glances over making a soft smile then looks at her watch. 'We should drink these quickly; the first set will be playing shortly.'

They walk to the harbour, noticing the intensity of people buzzing all around them.

As they enter The Hunt, the bar is full of excitable, drunk expats. Lily and Sara feel the electric energy pulsating throughout the room. They make their way through swarms of people, edging closer to the bar. When they finally get the bartender's attention, Lily orders two tequilas, and hands one back to Sara who is standing just behind her. 'Cheers.'

Lily lifts up her glass and responds, 'Cheers, here is to a good night!' Without hesitation she orders another two beers.

They sit down on the bar stools facing each other, ignoring the activity all around them, too deep in conversation, talking about their life in Australia, the challenges of being far away from family and friends. As the conversation flows, so does the alcohol. Lily's night off from work is an opportunity for her to forget her worries.

Their conversation is interrupted by an attractive man who begins to outwardly flirt with Sara. Lily gives them their space to chat and takes a moment to herself to relax into her seat. She nurses an ice-cold beer in her hands and directs the attention to the cover band that have started to perform on the stage. As if on autopilot her habit of drinking, ordering, drinking another comes into play. Before too long she has consumed a toxic mix of tequila and beer.

Without warning, flashbacks, strong flashbacks become more prevalent, highlighting a much darker time in her life. The flashbacks are in laser sharp focus, playing a familiar scene. She is triggered; her body is in a state of shock, her breathing quickens. Lily violently shakes her head to dispel the memory, but it doesn't shift. The alcohol hangs heavily over her as does the noise of the live music that is now beating aggressively in the background. She normally loves the energy of the music, but tonight it is too overwhelming.

The flashbacks play through her mind, as a movie, vivid and uncomfortable. The intensity is making her mind and body believe that she is back at a party in London, A party Lily had attended after just losing her mum. That night she went with the intention of seeking some light relief; the reality was very different.

The movie continues with another scene that races and overlaps into the next scene, before it even has a chance to end; moment after moment, distant and faint thoughts blur with no time to think clearly.

Lily's body triggers into a fight or flight scenario; heart racing, pounding through her white t-shirt, hot flushes shooting through her body. Lily sits at the bar, head in hands, totally zoned out of reality and into the nightmare which lives is her inner world. Her own painful reality.

She cannot bear to relive the scene again so, without hesitation, orders two more tequilas and drinks them one after another, this is the drinking to oblivion spoken about with Mr. Lint, the need to numb her emotions, trying to forget her traumas.

Lily exhales deeply and looks over to Sara for reassurance but she is still engrossed in conversation with her handsome companion. Every now and then, Sara does turn back to check in with Lily, totally unaware of what is truly going on.

Lily feels her phone buzzing through her denim shorts. It's Charlie. Ignoring the call, she places the phone back into her pocket. Slowly, surely, the effects of the alcohol take its fierce control. The room begins to spin around Lily as she falls off her bar stool. Stumbling through the crowd, she bumps, nudges into people as she heads for the centre of the dance floor. The surrounding crowd all turn and face Lily, watching her as she sways, standing with her eyes closed, her blond, messy locks shift all around her. Her attention is now on the strong beat of the music, the vibrations of the bass awakening her senses, she begins to move her hips to one of her mum's all-time favourite songs, it's a rendition of Daryl Hall and John Oates *Man eater* that pulses through the band's speakers. Lily moves and listens to this familiar song, which is both heart-breaking and comforting.

She remembers her mum and begins to imitate the way she would move, gliding around the kitchen. With her eyes firmly shut, Lily desperately wants more than anything to be back together with Paul and her parents, but the harsh reality is that there will never be another moment, a moment when they can all be together as a family.

Lily keeps her mum alive through her thoughts and memories, which is all she can do. The realisation of her reality is distressing.

As she opens her eyes, she is now aware of the surrounding people that are all glaring towards her. Needing to be alone to process the pain and torture, she races over to Sara, and lets her know that she will be leaving.

The cool night air hits her warm cheeks, making her feel dizzier and more unsteady. She walks over and sits on a bench that overlooks the harbour. In a daze, she opens her phone to see a couple of texts from Charlie.

'Hey Lils, you OK, still coming over tonight? x' Sent at 8:10 pm.

Then another text at 11:20 pm. 'Going to bed soon, hope you and Sara are having fun, text me later so I know you have got home safe, night babe x'.

Lily doesn't respond, instead she looks out towards the boats that are moored in the harbour and fixes her gaze on the midnight light that is reflecting off the calm waters, shimmering, almost sparkling.

Chapter 9

Sam follows Olivia into the bar, scanning her every move. His admiration is bordering on obsession. He notices every detail, how she saunters confidently, her tailored clothes that are tightly wrapped around every curve, he is becoming desperate, craving, to see what lies beneath. The bar is dimly lit, intimate, the perfect setting for romance, he thinks. Candlesticks flicker on wooden high tables and chairs. The clientele is mostly couples or women enjoying an after-work drink with colleagues.

They find an empty table in the corner. Sam attempts not to seem distracted, 'What would you like to drink?'

Olivia shoots a seductive glance, 'A Merlot would be great, thanks.'

Sam notices the look and begins to flirt, 'Miss Bloom, will that be a small or large?'

Olivia doesn't need to respond, instead she gives an enigmatic smile.

'A large then'

They are away from prying eyes, no colleagues, or familiar faces around. The bar may be full of customers, but with no one judging them, Olivia and Sam feel able to express their true feelings.

After a long intense moment of silence, Olivia takes a large sip of wine then places the glass on the table. Her smile illuminates her face, 'Well done again, you were great in the meeting.'

'Thanks, it was very much a team effort. I think Isla was impressed. The visuals and pitch were really strong.' He continues, 'I couldn't have done it without you.'

Olivia bites her lip, 'So, how are you finding York, is it everything you expected? Do you not miss all the fun and excitement back in London?'

Sam thinks about the question for a while. His life in the last couple of weeks has taken some unexpected turns but the truth is that being with Olivia is the most excited he has felt in a long time, questioning whether it is because it is so different from his daily repetitive, mundane life. Whatever the reason he never imagined or wanted to be attracted to anyone else outside of his marriage to Francesca.

But Olivia has unintentionally become the full focus of his thoughts and actions. When they aren't together, he can't stop thinking about her, where she is, what she is doing. This is now transitioned from being just a playful crush; the extent and depth of his emotions have crossed over into a deep, dark, dangerous obsession.

'Well, it depends.'

'On what?' Olivia answers.

'What areas you are talking about. The work element is unsurprising, the job at New Dawn being with the team and work is everything I thought it would be. Then everything else is…'—there is a long pause—'unexpected and surprising!'

Olivia seems confused. 'Oh,' she states.

'I suppose what I am trying to say is that I didn't expect to meet someone,' Sam responds.

Olivia eyes widen, piercing her focus intently at Sam, listening as he continues.

'Someone I barely even know but can't stop thinking about. All I keep asking myself is, does she feel the same?' With every word, Sam speaks slowly, with intent he leans his body in closer to Olivia.

She has sensed the connection ever since their first encounter at the welcome dinner at Gabrielle's. She takes a while to respond. 'It doesn't matter how I feel, or how you feel, the fact is you are married and if it would be wrong to explore anything?'

Sam shakes his head, in an almost frustrating manner. 'I know, like I said I didn't expect this and trust me it would be a lot easier if I never met you. I didn't know it was possible for me to feel this way for someone else.'

Olivia is confused, not knowing how to respond. Eventually, she asks, 'Have you had these feelings outside of your marriage, for someone else, before me?'

Sam takes a moment to respond, he looks down to the table, facial expressions portray a small frown, "No, not like this. Of course, I have been tempted, but I do love Francesca, she is a great mum, supportive wife, she gave up everything. Her career, her life, moved to York for me, my job."

Olivia sits back in her chair, confused, anxious. She cares about Sam deeply, but her strong moral compass is yelling the danger and consequence of what could happen when you fall for a married man. Yet just looking at Sam, hearing his confusion, she feels torn about what to do.

In the most genuine tone, Olivia begins to softly communicate, 'I am sorry about that, all of this. This just isn't me. I have never been a woman to think about running off with a married man and have an affair. It's not right and nothing good can come from this. As much as I am… tempted.'

Sam's eyes light up. 'You are?'

'Well, yes. I mean I didn't expect to feel this way either. I haven't had a relationship for about two years, so this is new for me as well.'

Olivia has never mentioned her ex before, so the mention of previous relationships intrigues Sam; needing to know more. 'Whatever happened with your ex then?' asking inquisitively.

Olivia's eyes showcase a great sadness, she lets out a sigh. 'Where do I start? I met my ex, Harry, Harry Akington, seven years ago at a property dinner. We were together for about five years. It was great, I loved him, but there were obstacles that, in the end, drove us apart. It was heart-breaking but we are probably better off as friends.'

'Obstacles?' Sam responds.

'Yes. I wanted kids, so badly wanted kids but it isn't something Harry saw in his life. As heart-breaking as it was for us both, I had to leave. Maybe we just weren't meant to be.

'Leaving him, is that something you regret now?'

Olivia continues, 'I am not sure. All I know is that we are still best friends and have so much respect for each other. No matter what happens in life, I can rely on him, knowing he will always be there.'

Sam can't comprehend being friendly with an ex, maybe because all his previous relationships before Francesca have ended in disaster.

'I am sorry to hear that,' Sam answers. He wanted to know more about Harry, his character. 'Do you still see him now?'

'Yes, all the time. As I said we are so close, nothing will ever change that.'

'In the two years you have been single, have you dated anyone else then?' Sam asks, sipping his wine, trying not to seem too fixated on her every word.

'Well, there have been the classic disastrous dates where friends have tried to set me up. I think with every disappointing date I become more content, used to the idea of being on my own. It would be great to meet someone but if I don't, that's OK too. I am pretty happy'.

Olivia looks lost within her own world, analysing herself, 'I am happy, lucky to have created a life that I love, focusing on what matters to me, my friends, family, work.'

Sam wants to ask where he fits into her life but instead, his thinking is interrupted as Olivia says, 'Anyway, my round. Fancy another drink?'

Sam remains silent and nods. His obsession takes a strong grip of his thinking patterns, desperate to know if he is an important part of her life. Wanting her to want him. Wanting her to need him. He is now no longer considering the consequences or repercussions of what this could mean for his family.

Olivia heads back to the table, as she places the wine down on the table in front of Sam, he acts on impulse and places his hand immediately on top of hers.

At his touch she takes a deep inhale, totally off guard by his approach. Heart racing.

Her gaze looks up to his and she quietly questions, 'What are you doing?'

'I don't know. This is wrong and complicated, I am married, and we work together but I can't stop thinking about you and know you feel the same.'

'So what happens now?'

Sam demands insistently, 'Come here.'

With Olivia still standing, Sam pulls her hips in between his legs. His left hand moves her hair behind her ears. She leans in as Sam edges forward, he wraps his hands around her long hair and uses the grip to pull her head to the side, he kisses her cheek as her body shivers. Olivia closes her eyes, in ecstasy, his lips then desperately search for hers, they embrace passionately, oblivious to people watching them.

After a long moment of intense passion, Olivia moves her lips away, breathless and flustered. Her eyes looking back at Sam, even more deeply, she stands there in his firm embrace, noticing every speckle in his eyes, the shape of his face. She moves her hand and slowly touches a birthmark on his neck, totally captivated, powerless to this man.

Chapter 10

Lily sways around the harbour bench, slowly sobering up, and her tired eyes closing. She takes her phone out of her pocket and immediately dials Charlie's number. No response. She calls again; unaware the time is now past midnight. Frustrated that he is not picking up, Lily doesn't think rationally, instead she acts on impulse. She jumps up from the bench and walks towards the taxi line, giving the driver Charlie's address in Bondi Beach.

The night sky changes to a dark purple. On the way to Bondi Beach, Lily leans her head on the window, head continuing to pound.

She drifts off to sleep, only to be woken by an irritated taxi driver.

'Excuse me. Excuse me, Miss, we have arrived.' His tone is loud and direct.

Lily wakes in a confused daze, forgetting where she is. Fumbling for the car handle, she nearly falls out of the taxi. As soon as the car door is slammed shut, the taxi speeds off leaving Lily in the middle of the road. Catching her breath, steadying herself onto her feet she takes short, slow, steps towards Charlie's front door. Still swaying, she knocks with one hand and uses her other hand to hold onto the door frame, keeping herself still. Another knock but no answer. A more dominating knock follows and still nothing. With the mixture of emotion and alcohol, Lily is unaware as she shouts, 'Charlie!' She falls onto the doorstep with a loud, encompassing thud.

Moments later, Lily can hear noises stirring from inside the house. Charlie opens the door, looking sleepy, dressed in his pyjama shorts, dishevelled and tired. 'Lily, what on the earth are you doing here?' he questions.

'Do I need a reason? I just wanted to see you, that was all' Lily asks impatiently.

'Of course not, it is just late, and I have work tomorrow.'

Disappointed with his response, she says still firmly crouched on the doorstep, 'OK, don't worry about it, I will go then.'

'Don't be silly. Here let me help you up.' Charlie stretches out his hand for Lily to grab. She holds onto him tightly as he pulls her up and nestles into his chest as they walk into the house and up to Charlie's bedroom. Lily walks into the bathroom, splashes her face with some cold water and looks back at her reflection in the mirror. Water droplets drip off her eyelashes, down onto her cheeks, she remains motionless judging her hazy appearance, how her eyes are glazed over, the result of an unhealthy mix of alcohol, tiredness, and emotion. Lily rests her hands onto the side of the sink not liking the woman she sees before her. She splashes water one more time and uses her hands to wipe away the excess dark, makeup residue.

The morning light pours onto their faces; the warmth of the sun gently cradles Lily, waking her up.

She coyly says, 'Morning.'

'Morning, babes,' Sam responds in his endearing Northern tones, with his eyes still shut.

Unsure of how Charlie will respond to last night's antics, Lily coyly attempts at an apology, 'Look, I am sorry about last night. I didn't mean for this to happen. I just wasn't thinking, I was drunk and wanted to see you, that is all it was. I should have thought, but i acted on impulse.'

'Honestly, it is OK Lils.' He blinks his eyes open, to see Lily, wide eyed and frightened looking directly towards him. Acknowledging her clear anguish, he compassionately says, 'Everything OK? What's going on, talk to me?'

Lily shuffles into Charlie's embrace, resting her head on his chest, feeling comforted, protected.

'You know you can always talk to me,' Charlie reminds her.

'I know that. I just find it overwhelming. I am not much of a talker. Well, I am, but not about my feelings!'

'I like you. I am here if you want to open up to me.'

'Thanks for saying that. I do want to.'

Charlie squeezes Lily tightly, 'Good, you can trust me,'

Lily listens, hearing his heart echoing, beating, faster.

With a sense of sheer relief, a tear falls onto his bare chest. Charlie pulls her face inwards and kisses her lips.

Lily in her own unique manner reassures him, 'I know I can, I do want to get closer to you…I really do. I am just working through a lot.'

'I feel like you have built these walls around you, guarded. I want you to let me in, you can trust me,' Charlie requests.

Their conversation is abruptly interrupted by the fierce alarm buzzing, vibrating on the bed side table. Charlie reaches over, and slams it off, 'I must get ready for work. Are you at the Tap Bar tomorrow night? If not fancy dinner in Darling Harbour?'

Lily wipes her salty tears away and says, 'Actually, I have a night off and a date night sounds great!'

They walk out of the house together in the early morning light, say their goodbyes and part ways. Lily takes the bus heading towards home, sitting there, she watches the world fly past as she replays over the morning conversation with Charlie. She thinks that no matter how this love story ends she is grateful for a man that can confidently show strong empathy and compassion.

Charlie makes her feel secure, which helps build her own confidence. She becomes more excited than ever to see him and maybe even let him see a glimpse of her true self, all her complexities and fears, a side which, to date, has been hidden. Hidden from everyone.

She changes for her date night, wearing her favourite maxi dress and tanned waist belt. Even though it has only been a day since she last saw Charlie, she has missed him. As she strolls into the Rib and Grill Steakhouse, Lily is filled with a curious mix of emotion, apprehension and excitement.

She sees Charlie in the corner of the room on a small round table looking down at his phone, frantically typing away.

'Hey' Lily says, trying to sound confident as she approaches the table.

'Sorry, babe, just had to finish off an email. So glad it is Friday, and I am here with you.'

Always the gentleman, he stands up to welcome her, softly kissing her blushing cheeks. Walking around the table to pull out her chair, Lily is reminded of the old-fashioned chivalry she witnessed between her mum and dad. She smiles to herself, feeling content that standing in front of her is someone she can be proud to be with.

Charlie begins the conversation, 'I love this place; we came here for our first date. That feels like forever ago now.'

'Oh, does it?' Lily responds, confused of the context.

'What I meant to say is it feels like I have known you for a long time.'

The waiter comes over to take their drink order, Charlie looks over to Lily and asks, 'Shall we get a bottle of wine?' Lily nods.

'A bottle of the Malbec, please.'

As the waiter walks away, Charlie reaches out to hold Lily hands on top of the table.

Lily coyly begins, 'I have been thinking a lot, about the other morning and our time together. The way you are with me just makes me feel so comfortable.'

He doesn't respond, instead actively listens to Lily, giving her the space to continue talking.

'I never expected to meet anyone, especially not travelling and have been single for so long so this all feels so new to me,' she continues, 'And you are different, Charlie.'

'Different? In what way?' He asks.

'In every way I suppose. I grew up with such loving parents. Seeing the way they behaved with each other, made me so self-assured and confident that I would find someone that treated me in the same way. I suppose it made me believe that unconditional love was, is possible.'

Charlie softly strokes her hands with his thumb. 'Of course, it is.' Lily fidgets and looks down at their hands intertwined, unsure whether he was talking in general terms or directly about their relationship.

He senses an uneasiness, 'You never talk about your parents?'

'There isn't much to say, what do you want to know?'

'Everything, Lils. I want to know all about you, your life, childhood.'

Feeling supported and safe, Lily relaxes into the conversation. 'My brother still lives in our hometown in Surrey. He seems settled in his long-term relationship, has a house, a kid on the way. My dad on the other hand still seems lost. I suppose we are similar in that way.'

As the words fall out of Lily's mouth, she thinks about this idea of being lost, how she believed travelling would be the answer to help her find herself again after a long time.

'Dad has been single ever since my mum passed away. I wish that he would meet someone, but it hasn't happened, not yet. We all tried to find some normality after mum died, but the reality is, it's hard and it changed everything.'

With compassion Charlie responds, 'I am sorry to hear that. I can't imagine what you have been through.'

'Thanks. It was tough. When everything happened, I was so young. I don't think it matters what age you are when you lose a loved one. I mean we all need a mum, that maternal figure to guide us through this thing called life. I think we believe our parents are invincible, that they will always be there to protect us from everything. Sadly, I learnt so many years ago that it isn't true.'

The waiter interrupts the flow of the conversation to pour the wine. 'Are you ready to order?' he asks politely. Lily and Charlie look down at the menu one more time and confer.

'Yes, I think so. Please can I have the burger and skinny fries,' Charlie responds.

'I will have the same, thanks,' Lily says.

Charlie continues the conversation, 'How does your dad and brother cope with everything now?'

'A lot better than me, I think. After everything happened, I took on the responsibility to look after them as I felt they needed me. It was quite natural for me to adopt a more maternal role. I focused my attention on them. It kept me busy. Looking back, I don't know if that was my coping mechanism, to not be reminded of our new, painful reality.'

'That's OK,' he reassures Lily.

'I suppose so but in looking after everyone else, I neglected myself, it all became very overwhelming.'

Lily shakes her head in despair, her eyes become teary. She struggles to get the words out, 'I turned to alcohol then on one occasion drugs, all an attempt to numb the pain and quieten the noise in my head.'

Charlie looks on with amazement at Lily, so much so she becomes self-conscious and asks, 'What is it?'

'I think this is the first time since we met, you have opened up and been truly vulnerable with me.'

Lily lets out a small smile, 'Yes, it probably is. This is all new for me. I usually push away people that are getting too close, terrified of getting hurt.'

Charlie looks deeply into her eyes, tilts her head and responds lovingly, 'I am not going anywhere.'

Lily looks back, as if it is the first time since they met that she really sees the depth and pureness in his heart.

Chapter 11

That first kiss in the wine bar takes over, intoxicating Sam. He just can't get enough. Over the next few days all he can think about is the memory of the kiss with Olivia, how the electricity sparked and shocked his entire body.

He wants Olivia but to what extent, he doesn't know. If they take the relationship further, it would mean entering further into dangerous, uncharted, waters. He needs time to think of the next move but working together means the distance between them is only going to get significantly smaller.

A week after the pitch, Robert calls Sam and Olivia into his office.

'Hey team, I have news,' he states proudly as he walks around his office with his head held high, while Sam and Olivia sit on neighbouring chairs opposite his desk.

'So, team I have just received call from Isla Bourne. She was very impressed with you both. She specifically highlighted your initiative in proposing a concept outside the box. She also mentioned the chemistry between you and would be more than happy to appoint you as her architects on the project.'

Sam's gazes at Olivia, she feels his presence and looks back at him.

'Well done. I don't have to tell you the importance of Isla Bourne as a client and this scheme for the firm. Rumour has it she will be rolling out several large-scale developments, so impress her with this and additional business could potentially follow. I believed in you both and you delivered, so well done.'

'Thank you,' Olivia responds confidently to Robert.

As they walk out of Robert's office, Olivia turns to Sam and asks, 'Let's get together later tonight and discuss the next steps. Why don't you come over to mine at say 7 pm and we can talk.' A burst of adrenalin runs through his body, blood rushing to his face. They walk over to their prospective desks, Sam's phone pings with a message from Olivia sending her home address.

Sam immediately texts Francesca to inform her of the project's win and that he will not be home for dinner.

The hours to 7pm travel by slowly as Sam impatiently waits for them to be reunited. Thoughts of them together run through his mind ending with pleasurable fantasies of how the night may end.

As he walks up to Olivia's front door, he takes a moment to notice the terrace Victorian house, small patio at the front and big bay window. After knocking nervously, hands shaking, Olivia opens the door, with her beaming smile. There is a confident glow around her. She is dressed down in grey joggers and an oversized navy sweatshirt seductively draping over her curves. Sam eyes travel all over her body.

As Olivia invites him in, Sam is welcomed by a sweet essence of garlic and butter filling the kitchen.

'I didn't know if you would be hungry but I've made some dinner for us, just in case you are,' Olivia says softly.

'That's kind. It smells great, thanks, Liv. Is it OK if I call you Liv?'

Olivia turns to Sam and just smiles.

Sam instantly makes himself at home and sits at the dinner table. He takes a deep inhale of the sage scented candles that are flickering in the kitchen, lighting the room in soft, warming colours. Her house is cosy and inviting, there are no loud noises of kids crying and children's toys covering the floor. Sam instantly feels calmer as Olivia serves a home cooked butter baked cod and steamed greens. They engage in conversation firstly about the scheme, what is needed and where the responsibility sits within the project. Very quickly the conversation becomes more personal, more intimate.

'Thanks for making dinner, this is great. I want to say that the other night in the wine bar was amazing, I haven't stopped thinking about it,' Sam states.

'I know, I feel the same,' Olivia says flirtatiously.

They continue to eat, comfortable in each other's presence.

Once finished, Sam picks up the empty plates and takes it over to the sink to wash up. Olivia follows him to the sink, stands behind him and confidently grabs his waist.

'This is wrong, we shouldn't be doing this,' she says but then places her lips onto his neck, caught up in the smell of his cologne and the overwhelming intensity of her feelings, she kisses him, repeatedly. She pushes her chest against Sam's back, arms wrapped around him, she feels his stomach rise and fall, her breathing getting quicker with every kiss.

Sam's head falls back. They stand there enjoying the pleasure of holding each other.

Sam turns around to face Olivia. The sexual tension between them is palpable. Sam moves forward to kiss Olivia, slowly, then quickly, his hands run under her sweatshirt, around her body, feeling every inch of her curves. They continue to kiss as his hands head down her thighs, finding the drawstring on her joggers and unties the knot, as it slowly falls apart. They loosen, he grips the top and pulls them down. As her clothes hit the floor, it is a sign of the trouble and destruction that is about to follow.

Sam knows these moments of passion will cause upset and devastate his family unit. As thoughts of the consequence enter his mind, he deliberately pushes them back. The passion and danger of their blossoming affair overpowers any feeling of remorse or guilt.

Sam pushes the cookbooks and chopping board on the kitchen counter out of the way to make space, lifting her up and placing her bottom on the edge of the unit. Olivia takes off her sweatshirt and unclips her bra. Sam doesn't say a word as he looks down taking in every inch of her, capturing her magnificent figure. She falls back and lies seductively on the counter, looking up at Sam. He crouches down to kiss her ankles, calves, knees, in-between her thighs and all around the outline of her black, lacy, briefs. He stands up again, pulls her underwear down which slips off her toes onto the floor, landing on top of the joggers.

Olivia's excitement builds as she makes herself more comfortable on the kitchen counter. Sam is still fully clothed; he doesn't take his eyes off Olivia as he starts to throw off his clothes, pulling his cable knit jumper over his head revealing a strong, chiselled torso. Olivia stares at the naked areas of him she hasn't seen before, only fantasised about. Her desire builds; she pulls firmly on the belt of his jeans and draws Sam closer. His hands grab hold of the buckle clasp to yank it apart, then forcefully pulls his jeans and boxers downs over his feet and onto the floor. Sam takes hold of Olivia's hand, pulling her to him. She sits up, her pert bottom still on the edge of the kitchen counter. He runs his hand over her exposed breasts, then down into her thighs, beginning to caress her most intimate parts, Olivia's legs grip tightly around Sam's body, wanting every inch of him. Her body writhes in anticipation with every touch. When Sam feels that she can't take much more, he moves his body closer to the counter, pulls her body towards him and enters her. As soon as he does, he exhales; he is now in the longed-for state of total nirvana.

Different tempos and motions, his full body repeatedly thrusts into her. As their hot, sweaty bodies connect he watches over her. Olivia's face is lying on the counter groaning, moving around the counter as she silently screams with pleasure.

Finally, after a strong, intense act of passion, Sam collapses on top of her, finishing, all his energy released from his body. His body and mind empty, if only for a moment. There is a long pause of silence before he looks at his watch to notice the time is past 10pm. He knows he must leave and head back to reality. A reality that is pale in comparison to the intensity of this experience with Olivia. He launches himself off the counter, rumbles around to find his clothes that are scattered across the floor. Olivia lays there naked, eyes closed, perspiration glistening from her golden body.

No words are spoken between them, just feelings of expelled energy and exhaustion. For the first time, Sam begins to feel a twinge of regret and guilt, knowing that he must go home and face Francesca.

Sam puts his clothes back on and quietly whispers, 'That was incredible. I can't believe it, but I need to go. I wish it wasn't like this but hope you understand. I will see you tomorrow in the office.'

Olivia struggles with the idea that after sharing the most intimate moment, he is now going to leave her and crawl back home, into his marital bed. Thinking about Sam being with his wife and family makes her self-conscious and vulnerable. She jumps off the counter and desperately fumbles around for her clothes, feeling great sadness. She wants him, not only for a quick fuck but wants him, every part of him.

Watching Sam climb into the back of the taxi is shattering, she has given this man, her body and full heart.

As the taxi travels to his house, Sam mind replays every second of the evening, wanting to relive it all again. Feeling the electric passion between them, how she made the first move and kissed him, how her skin felt on his body, how his body felt inside her. He wants to do it all over again, hold her, kiss her thighs, pull her hair back. For now, all he has are memories and possibilities for the future to hold onto.

Nearing home, he hopes Francesca is asleep. He needs to shower quickly and get into bed without waking her up or raising any suspicion, but before he even has the chance to put his keys into the door, Francesca opens the door to him, she is still up, writing a cover letter for a role that has just been posted. She greets him warmly. Sam kisses her cheek before racing upstairs to shower.

Entering the bathroom, he takes off his clothes. Looking down at the pile of clothes creates a flashback of both his and Olivia's clothes mixed on her kitchen floor. He turns on the shower, closes his eyes and lets the water run down his body, cleansing him, and washing away guilt that lingers from the sins he has created.

He crawls into bed, exhausted, head crashing down onto the pillow. He feels a warm body climb in bed and affectionately wraps around him. Francesca asks, 'How was work, all OK? I am worried; you are just working so hard.' Sam doesn't respond. She continues, 'I feel like I never see you, it would be nice to spend some together, how about I organise a date night for us if we can find a babysitter for the kids?' Sam nods, shrugging his shoulders upwards, giving a little smile. 'Good idea. Night, Cesca.' He kisses her lips and immediately turns over, wanting to be somewhere else, anywhere else.

Chapter 12

The morning after their date night Lily makes herself her a coffee, she cradles it, warming her hands. She rarely sees 9 am at the weekend but in this moment, she feels peaceful and content. She leans against the patio doors, taking a sip from the hot coffee, looking out onto the garden. The warmth of the coffee and the sunshine on her face soothe, relax her. She thinks about Mr. Lint and the support he has given her, paired with the compassion Charlie is showing. Lily realises how proud she is of this new journey she is on. A path where she is finding her inner strength and voice.

The following Wednesday, Lily takes the familiar journey to Mr. Lint's office. As the weeks pass by, Lily is becoming more willing to open and share her life story with him, edging closer to face her fears and demons that lie within.

The therapy sessions that once provoked overwhelming anxiety are now a space where Lily is starting to see a better version of herself, evolving. For ten years, she has felt a prisoner to her own anxious thoughts, living in her internal world overpowered by fear, a place she has occupied for a third of her life. Fear of the unknown, fear of losing someone she loves, fear of never finding another person to truly love her. Fear of feeling unsafe and not being able to handle it. Fear of not speaking her truth.

There were still other fears she knew she would probably have to face in time; but her mind is becoming clearer, the vision of her future now looking brighter, her heart more open to welcome in true love.

She takes the lift to reception, sits down in a chair, and calmly reads through the magazines, patiently waiting for Mr. Lint.

Mr. Lint walks and invites Lily into his therapy room. Her attitude, demeanour is different. She doesn't fall onto the couch and fling her bag down like she usually does. Instead, she takes her tanned jacket off and folds it neatly on the couch, puts her handbag on the floor and sits down on the edge of the couch, crossing her legs.

'Morning, Lily.'

'Hi.' Lily smiles as she responds, her tone upbeat and relaxed.

Mr. Lint recognises a shift in Lily so asks inquisitively, 'Forgive me for saying this but you seem different?'

'Do I? In what way?'

'In many ways, your energy seems calmer, more relaxed.'

'I am glad you sense that. I do feel calmer.'

'That is great to hear, I can see a difference. So, let's get started. How has it been since I last saw you?'

'A lot has happened this week. It started a bit shaky I suppose. Sara and I went on a night out, we were sitting at the bar drinking. Drinking too much. I knew that at the time, but I was all in my head, so many noises and thoughts bouncing around, so I resorting to my coping tool, drinking. The alcohol usually helps to quieten the noise but this time it didn't. I just felt worse, so I left the bar, totally wrecked. I was ringing Charlie, couldn't get through to him so on impulse I turned up at his house in the middle of the night.'

'So, you showed up to his house, drunk?'

'Yes'

'How did he respond?'

'The same way he always does, supportively. It didn't seem to faze him, nothing does.'

'OK.'

'After that, I don't know, something within me began to change. He makes me feel safe and secure. Usually when I get too close to someone, I run or push them away, but this time with him it feels different. That morning after we talked and he suggested a date night at our favourite restaurant on the harbour.'

Mr. Lint sits opposite Lily on his chair, legs crossed with a pen and paper in his hand, making notes.

'He knows I can be guarded but it doesn't worry him. In his kind way he pushes me to open to him and be vulnerable, I suppose.'

'We have touched on vulnerability before. If that is out of your comfort zone, how did it make you feel, opening yourself to him?'

'Terrified!'

'OK. Why is that do you think?'

'I don't know, I thought he would see the real me, my fragile side and not like it. I thought he would run away.'

'And has he?'

'No,' Lily responds immediately. 'If anything, it has bought us closer. I haven't felt like this in such a long time.'

'You should be proud of the progress you are making,' Mr. Lint says as he leans forward. He continues, 'Always remember that vulnerability creates intimacy.'

'What do you mean by that?' Lily asks.

'What I mean is that the more you can let your guard down, be who you really are with someone, you will not only attract the right person but will also have a more meaningful and deeper relationship.'

'Yes, I suppose you are right.'

'Great.' Mr. Lint glances through his notepad. 'Looking back at the notes of the previous session you mentioned an event that happened that still seems to affect you. We talked about the loss of your mum and the trauma that followed but when we were talking, it seemed there was something else, another event that has been a great source of anxiety for you. Is that right?'

Lily, wide eyed, sits completely still, staring at Mr. Lint. As if paralysed she does not say anything, only fidgeting slightly, feeling uncomfortable.

Mr. Lint doesn't say a word. If she wants to talk, she will; he knows not to push her too much.

The seconds tick away, the only communication coming is from Lily's body language.

Finally, she encourages herself to speak out. 'OK, I can do this.'

Lily looks at Mr. Lint. 'I want to tell you that in ten years I have never discussed this with anyone, not my dad, not my brother, not anyone.'

'My home is in a small village, in Surrey, England to be exact. It is really the most beautiful, quaint place. Full of character, it almost feels like you have stepped back in time, it is so picturesque, the village sits amongst green, rolling hills and the streets are lined with trees. A lot of the resident's commute from there to work in the City of London.'

Lily, deep in thought, continues slowly, 'It is quiet. There isn't much trouble, or problems that happen around there apart from the occasional rowdy night.' Lily's eyes start to dart around the room, unable to focus. She takes a long pause before continuing, 'But there was one night, where I happened to be in the wrong place, at the wrong time.'

Mr. Lint, intrigued by this new revelation, puts his notepad and pen down, leans forward, focusing on Lily and what she might say next.

'Let me start at the beginning. My mum had recently passed away. I was so caught up with her illness before she died that when she did pass, I became obsessed over organising everything, planning the funeral. I wanted to take the weight off Peter and Dad. The days around the funeral all rolled into one, I felt like I was in a waking nightmare. It was a month or so after the funeral, when all the planning and everything that needed to be done was over that I had time to really reflect. So, when I had the space to think about everything, the grief and trauma really struck me down, it was like a physical pain piercing my heart.'

Lily's eyes glaze over with emotion, tears streaming down her cheeks, voice cracking from the immense emotional load of the recollection.

Her voice rises in desperation and hurt, 'It hit me like a fucking truck. I was trying to pick up the pieces of my life that was now shattered into a million fucking pieces. There were times I would get in the shower, let the water run over me just so the noise could cover my suppressed screams. I couldn't relax, nothing seemed to be working, and there was no way for me to find a release. That is when the drinking became bad.'

Mr. Lint sits motionless wanting to capture the full essence of Lily's story and the true authenticity she is showing, 'All I could think was that mum wouldn't be proud of me, seeing me like this, gulping wine out of the bottle, but it became my medicine and from there everything spiralled. I started drinking more but that eventually stopped taking away the full extent of my pain. The pain felt debilitating, I needed it to disappear, but didn't know how.'

'It was a Friday morning, sometime in April. The mornings were getting lighter so I would get up early and come downstairs to make a coffee. Dad was already in the kitchen, he couldn't sleep. I suppose it was understandable as mum had only recently passed away. We were chatting away when Peter sent me a text, 'Party in Box Hill, it's a friend of Alex, fancy it? Alex will pick us up at 8 pm.' Alex is a friend of Peter's. At the time we were all in our 20s so house parties happened a lot, usually when parents were out of town.'

Lily stops talking, takes a moment to grab the bottle of water from her bag and takes a large sip. She puts the lid back on and grips the bottle tightly in her hands, so tight her knuckles are looking white.

'I really wasn't in the mood to socialise and answer any questions that people may have about mum but knowing I would be at the party with my brother made me feel a lot more comfortable and I did need to get out of the house and let my hair down. As I got ready for the party, I drank several vodka tonics in my bedroom. Looking back, I don't know how I had the strength to go, I was torn apart inside. Empty, hollow, numb.'

Mr. Lint senses her pain and hurt, knowing that whatever is about to be spoken is coming from a dark, hidden place within Lily.

Lily continues, 'Peter comes home after work, I hear him chatting to his mates in his bedroom next to mine. Talking about how it is going be to a big night and they were up for it. He dealt with the loss of mum in a very different way, he acted tough, strong. There were moments though where I would see straight through this and I knew he too was lost, like we all were. On the surface he remained this fun loving, party boy. There are 14 months between us, being the older sister, I felt such a responsibility to nurture him.'

'Alex picks us up in his brand-new car, a BMW. Growing up, I was surrounded by a lot of privileged kids. A lot of our childhood friends were from the private school we went to—The school—was very grand. Many of the kids that went there had parents successful in their field, who made a lot of money in banking, manufacturing, law, property, you name it.'

'We drove on the road up to Box Hill, which isn't far from our village. In Surrey, you really feel like you are in the countryside, many of the houses are spread out, sitting within large grounds. Some of the houses are unseen from the road, hidden by long driveways and iron gates. The party was in a sixteenth-century manor house with a big circular fountain spouting water at the entrance, which acted as a roundabout. Everywhere you looked the lawns and trees were manicured. It looked like a smaller version of a house from that TV show, you know, *Downtown Abbey*.'

Mr. Lint makes a slight smile and watches Lily as she continues to speak.

'The party was boring at the beginning, everyone drinking in the various rooms downstairs. The kitchen had a very traditional feel, dark oak floors, white painted cabinets, a big cooker. There were so many people in there, spilling out into the lounge. The house was like a maze, it was so old, a lot of nooks and crannies, doors that led off to other rooms. I sat talking to Peter, drinking more vodka. It's about 11pm; we had been there for several hours, just drinking. My head was starting to spin, eyes blurry and then…what then followed has stuck with me for ten years.'

She stops talking and looks down, hands continuing to grip the water bottle, face tense.

Mr. Lint does not want to stop Lily from talking but knows that he needs to centre and reassure her.

'Lily,' he says quietly. She looks up, terrified. 'This is really good but before we continue, I would like you to ground yourself and take a couple of slow, deep breaths, OK?' She nods her head. 'OK, in through your nose and out through your mouth,' he says calmly. Lily follows his directions, closes her eyes, and takes two very long, slow, breaths. The long out breath seems to flush some of the thoughts away. She opens her eyes, looking slightly more relaxed.

'OK. I am ready,' Lily says.

'All of sudden, this guy at the party that I was chatting to pulls out a bag of cocaine from his pocket. I was never into drugs. I would drink, at that point was getting hammered a lot, but that was it. For whatever reason I wanted to try it, see what it was like. See how it felt. All I knew is that I couldn't feel much worse than how I felt at the time. I watched him lay the coke on the kitchen table and shape the powder into perfectly formed horizontal lines. He turned to me asking if I wanted a line. I didn't even respond, without thinking, I bent over, finger to one nostril and snorted the first ice white line. The sensation was immediate, I threw my head back. I felt the inside of me come alive, my senses heightened, hyper focused. It must have been an hour or so later when everything became overwhelming, the mixture of vodka, cocaine, as well as trying to hide my true feelings, I felt sick, physically sick, my head was spinning out of control and wouldn't stop. People around me seemed to be blurry, rushing around, like a whirlwind. I needed space to be on my own, so I walked out of the kitchen, up a grand staircase and down a long hallway. Just like downstairs, the house had many doors to so many hidden rooms. I remember thinking it felt cold, stately, like living there wouldn't feel like living in a home.'

Lily sighs, face looking in despair.

'I found a bathroom, shut the door and locked myself in. I sat on the floor leaning against the bath, knees pushed up to my chest, resting my head onto my knees. I wanted to sob but couldn't, instead I focused on trying to steady myself and not be sick. I rocked slowly forward, trying to get my composure and thoughts together. And then…'

Lily looks back down on the floor; Mr. Lint waits calmly for Lily to continue her story and shake off the burden she has carried for so long.

'I heard sounds. I can't really describe them as they sounded muffled. I didn't know where the noise was coming from, I could hear a girl and guy's voice. The noises seemed to get louder. I held onto the bath for balance trying to stand up, it took a while. A few attempts later, there I was in the bathroom, room spinning around me. Vision blurred I searched for the door, unlocking it, and walked back into the long corridor. Hands on the wall, I listened for the sounds which projected from a room at the end of the corridor. I looked around, there was nobody in sight. I could hear loud music and people talking downstairs, but the noises started, again, clearer and sharper than before. I don't know what came over me, but I began to stumble towards the noise which were getting louder, more piercing, dominating, totally fucking uncomfortable.'

As soon as the words leave her mouth, Lily stops fidgeting, she freezes. Mr. Lint doesn't say a word; he gives her the time and space she needs to unravel, to uncover the truth. A truth that for ten years hasn't been spoken about.

Chapter 13

The affair is hidden from everyone in plain sight. With Sam and Olivia winning the Isla Bourne instruction, there isn't anything suspicious when Sam and Olivia leave the office to work on the project as Isla has the reputation of being meticulous and demanding. They devised a calculated routine to have time together allowing Sam to be at home around 7:30 pm with Francesca, just in time for dinner and for him to play the role of the doting husband and father.

Olivia's feelings become heightened, more than ever as she realises, she is beginning to become reliant on Sam and how he makes her feel when they are together. Whilst the moments they steal together are filled with joy, they are swiftly followed by utter devastation once again when Sam leaves her to go back to his wife and children.

The stolen time together was bliss. That all changed one afternoon. They meet at Olivia's around 4 pm, as the front door is shut, they frantically pull and grab at each other clothes. The raw chemistry is electric; Sam cannot get enough of Olivia, her touch, her body. She is becoming like a drug to him, one he now needs. For Olivia, the insatiable and longing that Sam shows her is like an aphrodisiac, one she is happy to indulge.

In the hallway as they take each other clothes off, he can't wait another moment. He must have her, now. In one quick movement, he pushes Olivia to the other side of the wall in the hallway and immediately unbuttons, takes off her silk shirt. Standing there in her seductive lingerie, Sam walks backward to get a full view of her body. He looks on in desire and breathlessly says, 'I will never get enough of you.'

The words arouse Olivia.

Olivia moves towards Sam, kissing his neck. She takes his trousers off and then her own underwear. They stand there naked, looking at each, breathing heavily in anticipation. They know the sensations they are about to enjoy and the thought of it heightens their excitement. Sam lifts Olivia's legs so they are now wrapped around him, walks over and places her on the stairs and lies on top of her. Sam always gets what he wants and he knows how much Olivia wants him. He enters her, slowly, teasing at first, then drives his body into her, deeper. Olivia on the edge of the stairs, rocks back and forward, moaning in pleasure. They kiss and bite each other's lips, as their movements quicken.

Sam's movements speed up, intensifies, he grabs, yanking her hair. The motion becomes quicker, he pounds harder, deeper, shifting her body around the stairs to achieve the maximum pleasure for himself and his own sexual gratification. As they continue, the line between pleasure and pain becomes quickly blurred.

Olivia gasps, 'Sam, stop, you are hurting me!' Sam ignores the plea and selfishly continues to fulfil his own needs. Olivia feels Sam's weight heavy on top of her, totally aware of how helpless she now is, she continues to wriggle underneath him, trying to move out of his grip, as she does his movements only continue to quicken, Sam continues to find his pleasure inside of her, oblivious, blinded to how uncomfortable she is feeling.

His climax expels all his excess energy, he feels alive and invincible, capable of achieving anything, ignorant to Olivia and the torment he just put her through.

She is totally shaken and in disbelief as to what just happened, lying still on the stairs, arms wrapped around herself as Sam gets off and starts to get dressed. Feeling so vulnerable and alone, she cradles herself and then races to put her clothes back on that are scattered all over the hallway. She is concerned about what just happened, how Sam had not listened to her plea to stop, something she had not witnessed before. This is the first time seeing an aggressive streak, it was alarming. Terrifying.

Unaware of this shift in Olivia's feelings, Sam continues to fumble around, getting dressed and looks for his phone, he sees messages and calls from Francesca, as well as a text message at 4:10 pm, 'Hey, where are you? Had to pick Nico up from school, he isn't feeling well, any chance you can come home early tonight, I need you to help out? X' Sam looks at his watch, it is now 6:15 pm. Sam knows he has to leave immediately.

He does not consider the repercussions of his affair, only the slight residue of guilt when jolted back to reality when Francesca and the kids enter his mind. He never thinks of the family and the damage he is causing when he craves Olivia. As much as he loves his kids, being with Francesca in their home does not fulfil all his needs in the same way that being with Olivia does.

He turns back to Olivia who is shaking as she rebuttons her blouse, staring down at the floor. Sam says disappointedly, 'Sorry, Liv, I can't believe it but I have got to run. There is a problem at home.' He kisses her cheek and whispers softly into her ear, 'That was fucking hot, same time tomorrow?' Olivia does not respond.

He calls a taxi as he waits on the path outside Olivia's house then immediately calls Francesca. 'Hi, darling, I was tied up in a meeting.' Sam says with no further explanation or apology given.

Francesca responds sounding panicked,' Where have you been, I needed you here, at home?' Francesca frantically shouts over the sounds of Nico and Bella crying in the background.

Irritation runs over Sam; not only has he left Olivia's early but he knows he will be returning home to chaos.

'Just relax. I am on my way, be there soon.' Still with no further context, he puts the phone down as the taxi pulls up. During the taxi journey, he prepares himself for all the questions Francesca may ask and thinks about his response. As soon as the taxi turns into his drive, Sam jumps out totally frazzled, already aware of the sounds from inside the house.

He opens the front door and hears Nico crying upstairs and Bella pushing her toy stroller and baby around, the wheels making a screeching noise as they run over the parquet flooring. Francesca slams the kitchen cupboards shut and walks into the hallway with a bottle of kid's medicine. Flustered, she looks over at Sam. 'Can you give 5ml of this to Nico, he is in his bedroom.' There is no response, so she repeats louder, 'Sam, please, I have a million things to do, once you are done, we have to talk.' She shoves the medicine into his hands and marches past Bella on her stroller and into the kitchen.

Giving medicine to his child is a normal request but still a sense of anger rushes over him without knowing why. He drops his bag and races upstairs to Nico's bedroom, sitting on the spaceship bedsheets next to him and says, 'All OK, pal? What happened then?'

'I didn't feel well at school, so Miss. Roberts sent me home.' Sam reaches over and uses the back of his palm to feel his forehead. 'Yes, you do have a temperature, here take some of this, this will make you feel better.' Sam pours the liquid onto the measuring spoon and feeds it to Nico. 'Get some sleep now, you should feel better in the morning.' He kisses his cheek and walks out of the room. He closes the door and stands outside taking time to reflect, he loves his kids more than anything, but something has changed. He is beginning to see Francesca in a different light, agitated at how dependant she is on him.

Francesca and Bella walk up the stairs. 'I am going to get Bella ready for bed,' she says, her voice trying to remain calm, but Sam knows from the look in her eye that she isn't happy with him. He showers and puts on his grey loungewear and heads to the kitchen, needing a drink. The kitchen is a mess. There are toys, papers, and the kid's homework everywhere. Searching the kitchen cupboard, he finds the bottle of Jameson and pours himself a large measure. He is trying to calm himself but is unreasonably becoming more furious of Francesca's demands. He is blinded to the fact that she is behaving normally; it is his perspective of the situation that has changed.

He stands looking out to the garden, just like he did the day they moved into the house but no longer appreciating the tall ceilings in their house or the big garden. York is a lot quieter than London but the inner turmoil in his head remains.

His senses return to the kitchen at the sound of Francesca saying, 'Nice of you to turn up then. I don't ask much of you, Sam, so when I say I need you, I mean it, and I need you here. I really don't think that is too much to ask, do you?'

Sam looks furious and stares out of the window, tensing his jaw, not saying a word. Francesca walks towards Sam and sees the anger on his face uncertain as to why he is acting this way.

Francesca is unable to get a response from him, 'Sam, what is going on with you? I haven't seen you all week, you are working late pretty much every night and the one time I need you, you aren't around to help?'

Sam still doesn't respond.

Feeling rejected, she says, 'Please, I don't ask for much.' Her voice breaks, the emotion visible to see.

Sam faces and turns to Francesca, anger projecting in his voice, 'What do you want from me?' He takes another large sip of whiskey. 'I am doing the best I can to win over my colleagues and nail the new scheme, there is so much pressure on me, I don't need this added aggravation when I come home.'

Francesca looks at Sam, her eyes well up with emotion, 'Aggravation? What are you talking about? Is it an unreasonable request for me to ask for your help in looking after our kids? What do you expect, for me to do everything all on my own?'

She tries to hold his gaze as her voice gets louder, 'We are meant to be a team. Listen to me please, Sam!'

Sam grips his glass, slamming it down on the kitchen counter, the alcohol in the glass tumbler spills over the sides at the force of the movement. Blood rushes to his face, he moves towards Francesca, holds out the palm of his hand and firmly uses his weight to push his hand into her chest.

Tensing his jaw, his eyes widen ashe shouts, 'Why are you are always nagging me. Can't you see that I am working late, I am doing all this just to benefit you and the family?'

Francesca sees Sam towering over her, he looks up at him becoming frightened. He continues to push against her, hard enough so that she falls back slightly, disorientated. Tears fill her eyes, heart beating, blood rushing through her body, she feels as if she is shrinking beneath him as Sam seems to grow taller, bigger, overpowering her. She stands there shaking, looking up at Sam who is staring, crouching over her. She doesn't recognise this man and thinks to herself, what happened to her Sam, the man she fell in love with? Where is he, where did he go? This man in front of her now feels like a stranger.

Tears roll down her face. She steps back slowly, away from him, not knowing what might happen next and as soon as she is a safe enough distance apart, she turns and runs up to the bedroom, slamming the door shut and locking it behind her.

Being with Sam had always been her safety net, he was someone she could trust and rely on. But the one person who used to make her feel as if she could achieve anything is now a stranger showing warning signs of aggression. She falls on to the bed, places her head into the pillow and screams, silently, releasing her fear, anger, hurt and heartbreak. She is bewildered, unsure of what to do next. She is living in a new city with no support system.

After a poor night's sleep, she wakes up fully clothed, not rested, and overwhelmed. Her head pounds, she turns to look at where Sam normally sleeps, noticing he isn't there. At that moment, she doesn't care where he is. Francesca knows she must shower and get ready for the day ahead, taking care of Nico and driving Bella to school. She walks over to the bathroom, looks at herself in the mirror, visibly noticing her red skin and puffy eyes, she sobs once more. For the first time since she met Sam, she is now unsure, uncertain of what their future looks like.

Chapter 14

'Can I just take a minute?' Lily asks Mr. Lint. He nods and lets out a sympathetic smile.

Lily takes a long sip of water and after a short break continues, 'OK, where were we? So, by now I am outside of this room where I think the noises are coming from. The corridor has an old musky wood smell, the noises from the party downstairs and from inside this room were overwhelming. I was still swaying and feeling, but then, suddenly, everything changed. The door to one of the bedrooms was ajar. I stood outside the door and peaked in. To this day I have thought and thought about what I saw that night and tried to make out the sounds more clearly, to piece together what was happening.'

Lily shakes her head and takes a deep breath before continuing, 'What I saw in the room was a man on top of this girl, having sex. I didn't see her face, just her naked body. I couldn't make out his face either, just his light brown hair with a slight wave to it and an unusual birthmark on the side of his neck. The man is using his hands to firmly press her down onto the bed. I stand in the doorway, frozen, something made me uneasy. I know I wasn't meant to be there watching but I was in utter shock. The next thing I remember is the guy pushing away from the woman, so there is more distance from their faces. He puts his hands around her neck. In my hazy vision, I see that he is putting more and more pressure around her neck.'

Lily puts her water on the floor and brings her hands to her head, talking into her hands, her speech is muffled and distressed, 'I stood there confused, unaware of how to feel, it made me so uncomfortable. I didn't know why but it didn't feel right. My perspective was warped because of the concoction of drugs and alcohol. I just didn't know what to do. I questioned whether to go in or leave them too it, not knowing if they were a couple and this was a normal part of their sex life. I just didn't want to get caught up in all of it. I felt paralysed, battling what I should do. And then it all got much worse…' Lily lets out a heavy sigh, her hands still covering her face, as if to guard, to protect herself.

'I left the party, I didn't say a word about it, went downstairs, I don't think I spoke to anyone, I must have looked like a zombie walking. It wasn't soon after when Peter came up to me to say he had booked a taxi, so we left. I went to the party to escape my life but instead that night has haunted me ever since.'

Chapter 15

Olivia stands in her hallway, buttoning her blouse over her bra. She watches Sam checking his phone before running out of the house. Her heart sinks, the aggression shown when they had sex has alarmed her, making her wonder whether she knows the real him. Standing alone, she feels disrespected and used. She is worth more than that, much more than how Sam has just made her feel.

Sam is the first man she has had a relationship with since her ex, Harry, but the situation is complicated, he is married with two kids, they work together and she is now confused about his actions in their recent sexual encounter.

She decides that the best thing for her is to create distance from Sam. Having reached this conclusion she makes an agreement with herself that all contact with him is held exclusively in the office. Communication will be solely focused on work.

It doesn't take long for Sam to sense that Olivia is pulling away from him. He can't take not being in control of his emotions. His emotions had continued to build until one day in the office he bursts out, 'What the hell is going on? Why are you ignoring me? We haven't been together for days.'

Olivia doesn't divulge the truth of how she is feeling and how violated he has made her feel so instead skims over the topic, looks him straight in the eye and says, 'This isn't easy for me either Sam but it's not right. It's not fair on anyone, not me, you, Francesca, the kids. Nobody wins in this situation.'

Sam looks puzzled; his eyes fixed onto her. 'Can't you see that none of that matters? I need you, Olivia!'

This sense of needing makes Olivia uncomfortable, as if he wishes to exert his control over her, once again.

More firmly she responds, 'This is not about what you want! There are other people to consider, including what I need. I have told you where I am, I enjoy working with you, let's just leave it at that before it gets more complicated. Anyway, we have the Isla Bourne scheme we should focus our attention on.'

Sam rests his hands on the table and Olivia notices his face getting noticeably redder with anger. Sarcastically, he responds, 'Fine if that's what you want.' Olivia takes back control of the situation and continues to change the topic.

That was it, the end of their romantic affair as they know it but the consequences of what they had already done was about to catch up with them.

A week later, Olivia walks home from work, just a typical Monday night. She loves her summer evening strolls, listening to a podcast, unwinding, thinking about the day. With the sun shining on her face, she makes sure to breathe in the floral scents of blooming flowers and freshly cut grass. She reflects on everything over the last month feeling pleased and empowered that she made the right decision to end her relationship with Sam, as enjoyable as it was, at times. She walks into her local, The Walnut Garden, a traditional pub, just minutes from her house, orders a cold beer and strolls into the beer garden. She takes a seat and lets the sun wash away any negative emotion that has been building up. Taking a sip, she relaxes further into her wooden seat and watches the people, listening to the sounds of talking and laughter all around. She sees the joy radiating from the parents' who are multi-tasking, engaging in conversation whilst always keeping an eye on their children who are playing on the climbing frame.

Olivia always imagined having a big family with the love of her life. For the years she was with Harry, Olivia believed this fantasy could be a reality. Harry seemed the perfect partner to build a family with. Whenever she thinks about what could have been her heart aches, still, even after all the time that has passed by.

Olivia leaves the pub with the sun almost disappearing into the horizon, just a small glimmer of sunlight as she walks home. Just as reaches her front gate, she sees a grey 4×4 parked in the distance, she squints to see a flash of light brown curly hair. It is Sam! She rushes to find the house keys that are clattering around her bag, hands shaking as she puts them into the lock and falls into the now open front door. She slips inside the house and immediately locks the door behind her. Dropping her bags, she runs upstairs to the spare bedroom which overlooks the front of the house and without turning the bedroom light on she peers through the window, looking down the road at the car. She can see Sam clearly who is eagerly staring at her front door. Her hands shake, heart fiercely beating, she feels uneasy and terrified. She remains watching him in the car until ten minutes later when he turns the car engine on and drives slowly past her house, looking out of his car window to try and get a glimpse of her. Olivia hides behind the edge of the curtain, watching as the car drives away. As soon as the car disappears into the distance, she falls back and slides down the wall until she is sitting on the floor. In total shock, she sighs heavily.

The morning after Olivia makes the decision to spend the day working from home, unable to go to work and face him, not knowing what to say. Why is he outside her house? How many times has he followed her? Why? What is his purpose? As these questions fill her mind, they make her anxious. She needs time to gather her thoughts and think about how to play this. She takes her phone from the bedside table and sends a text message to Robert, 'Morning, not feeling 100%, going to work from home today, hope that's ok. On my mobile if you need me.'

She sits in bed planning her Tuesday, opening the calendar on her phone, moving the internal meetings to conference calls. Scrolling through the month, she notices something strange. Her heart races, she jolts out of bed, shouting, 'No, that can't be right!' Frantically she goes back through her calendar, she realised it is true. She is late; it has been six weeks since her last period.

'Shit!' Throwing off the bed sheets she runs into the bathroom, opens the cabinets and anxiously sorts through the contents, pushing around cotton wall pads, toothpaste; make up brushes, to seek the one item she needs, a pregnancy test. There is usually an emergency one, just in case. This of course is an emergency. She finds it, nestled in a little blue wrapper. Olivia's shaky hands pick it up, as if in slow motion, her tunnel vision fixates on the test. Her future now lies on the impending results. Stomach churning, heart and mind racing with what the potential outcome will be, if is she pregnant, there is no doubt, the baby is Sam's.

Tearing the wrapper apart, she takes the test and places it on the windowsill and distracts herself by turning her attention to something else, anything else. The passing couple of minutes tick by painfully slowly.

Time is up, she bends over, eyes zooming in on the test and result. One vertical blue line appears clearly in the pregnancy test window, then another line. She is pregnant! Olivia's emotions turn into absolute turmoil. For so long she has wanted to be a mum with someone she loved, that has always felt like her true purpose but this situation is entirely different. The baby belongs to a man who is now stalking her and married with his own children. A cascade of feelings washes over Olivia. She falls to the floor, sitting there, confused and feeling incredibly alone. Who could she talk to about this with someone that wouldn't judge her? Immediately she pushes herself off the floor and runs over to her phone to dial Harry's number. She knows she will have to tell him everything. They confide in each other, their love life, disastrous dates, work, family, anything and everything. Olivia loves Harry deeply, as a friend and trusts his opinion implicitly.

Dialling his number, 'Pick up, Harry. Pick up, I need you.' Olivia says to herself, 'Harry!'

'Hey, Liv,' Harry answers in his usual calm demeanour.

'Harry, thank God you picked up, I don't know what to do, it's all becoming too much. I must chat to you, today. Are you around, what time can I come over?' Olivia asks frantically.

'Slow down, slow down. Liv, what's going on?' Harry senses her nervous energy.

'I can't explain now, are you at home?'

'Yes, I have a conference call in 15 minutes and then meetings with the team, want to come over at 1pm? I will make us some lunch.'

'Harry, thank you, see you later.'

When Olivia met Harry Akington seven years ago at the property dinner, she was attracted to him, his charm and how he made people feel so relaxed in his company. Even speaking to him now and given the situation, he puts her instantly at ease.

Olivia feels so lost in thought that she cancels all her meetings and runs a bath. Lying there she tries to ground herself, slowly breathing in the strong lavender aroma. Her mind wanders to visualising herself as a mum, thinking about what type of mum she would be, relaxed, fun, strict, anxious? She doesn't know. For the years when Olivia and Harry were together, she had thought about this endlessly, playing out imaginary scenes of their happy, healthy family.

Throwing on her joggers and sweatshirt she drives over to Harry's house. He opens the door and warmly greets her. She stands there for a moment, looking at him and swings her arms over him. Harry is taken by the affection but welcomes it in anyway, he rubs her back, she holds on tight not wanting to let go.

'Oh Liv, it looks like you have been crying. Come on inside, let's have lunch and you can tell me everything. Only if you want to?' Olivia nods, follows him and shuts the door.

Harry knows how to be with Olivia, truly be present in her company. Their five years together were magical; they were best friends, inseparable. Harry always wondered how they would have ended up if it wasn't for them having different views on starting a family. Since their breakup Harry tried to move on but can't, his heart still belonging to Olivia.

His biggest regret is never having children with Olivia. He has agonised over whether he should tell her. Tell her that he is now ready to be a father and the partner that she deserves, but to save their friendship he made the decision that it would be best not to discuss the topic. .

He walks into the kitchen. 'I made your favourite, goat's cheese and beetroot salad,' he says kindly, looking back at Olivia who is now sat on the kitchen table with her head in her hands.

She looks up slightly to say, 'Thanks, Harry, you are the best. I don't know what I would do without you.'

Harry notices that Olivia is in distress but allows her the space to talk to him.

He places the salads in front of them and sits down at the table to join her. 'Liv, you didn't sound happy on the phone, so I have given you extra croutons, I know how much you like them.' He takes a mouthful of food, Olivia stares down at the salad, picks up her fork and plays with the food, pushing the food around the bowl. Knowing that she isn't ready to talk, he changes the conversation. 'So, Liv, how is work? A friend of mine works with Isla. I believe she is very happy with you and is it, Sam? Seems like you both impressed her. Nice one, everyone knows that she is a tough nut to crack.'

Olivia ignores the question, deep in thought she finally responds, 'Actually, I don't know if I can eat this,' Olivia puts her fork down and continues, 'I need to tell you something. I really don't know how to say this, so I am going to start at the beginning. I have met someone, been seeing him for about seven weeks, it all happened so quickly, he took me by surprise, and I haven't felt this way since I suppose we were together.'

Harry is disappointed hearing that she is with someone else. Trying to seem supportive he replies, 'Happy for you, Liv, you deserve it.'

'It's not that simple, there are a number of factors that have made the situation complicated.'

Harry looks confused, 'OK.'

Olivia continues to talk, 'Please don't judge me.'

'I am always here for you, you know that. I will never judge you' Harry says reassuringly.

'We work together and he…'

There is a deafening silence between then, Olivia uncomfortably shifts in her seat. 'He is married.'

Harry stops eating, drops his cutlery and looks on intently. Olivia notices his dismay and continues, 'That isn't the half of it. It is much worse. I am pregnant with his baby and as if that isn't bad enough, I think he has also become slightly obsessed.'

His mouth and eyes are wide open. 'Ok, that is a lot of information to take in, what makes you think he has become obsessed?'

'Last night I went to the pub I just wanted to sit in the sun and have a beer, well, this was before I found out I am pregnant. As I am walking home, I see his car, parked up the road on the other side of the street. I ran upstairs to look out of the bedroom and saw him there, just sat in the car watching my house. It freaked me out. Harry, I don't know what I am going to do?'

Harry shakes his head, 'If you are dating then why would he need to stalk you?'

There is a tight, anxious look across Olivia's face, 'I finished the relationship'.

'You finished the relationship because he is married?'

Olivia shifts in her chair, 'Not quite. There was an encounter when I felt really uncomfortable with how he was treating me.'

'Ok. Have you called the police and told them?' Harry suggests.

'No, I haven't. I am so confused. And we work together which makes it more complicated.'

'This is tricky, Liv. I'll do everything I can to help, you know that.'

'Thank you so much, Harry. You don't know how much I appreciate your support and kindness.'

His tone changes, slower and quieter, 'I can't believe you are pregnant.' As he speaks Olivia can sense a great sadness pouring from him.

'I know, neither can I. I should have been more careful. I was just so caught up in the passion of it all.'

'What's this guy's name?'

'Sam.'

'Sam? You mean the same man you are working on the scheme with?'

'Yes. I know, I know. It is not ideal.'

'Let me see what I can find.'

Olivia enquires, 'What do you mean?'

Harry walks over to the kitchen counter, grabs his laptop and sits back down, pushing his half-eaten salad to the side.

'What is his surname? Where did he work before joining New Dawn?'

'Johnson, Sam Johnson. Atlas Architects in London.'

Harry types Sam Johnson into Google, a host of pages connected to Facebook and LinkedIn profiles pop up. He presses on the images tab. 'Is this him?' Harry turns the screen around to show Olivia.

'Yes, that's him.' Olivia can hardly look at the picture.

'Let me have a look, I want to see what he is all about,' Harry says, intrigued.

'How is that going to help the situation?'

'I don't know, but if he is acting strange and stalking you, then maybe he has done this sort of thing before?'

Harry sits there scrolling. 'Where is he from?'

'Surrey in London.'

Harry continues to bang on his laptop keyboard. 'Sam Johnson, Surrey,' he says to himself. The laptop screen highlights his eyes which are looking up and down on the screen as if he is scrolling through multiple internet pages.

'Harry frowns and shouts, What…What the hell is this?'

'What is it?' Olivia nervously asks.

'There is an article about a court case, ten years ago.' Harry's eyes quickly scanning the article. 'Seems like there was a party in Box Hill, Surrey where a girl aged 20 died.'

'Died? What? What has this all got to do with Sam?'

'Well from this article it is suggesting that he was the prime suspect. It says he was charged but there wasn't enough evidence to commit him. With no witnesses, the case never went to trial.'

'Charged? Court?' Olivia yells in total shock.

'Yes, the case has remained unsolved as there has been no further evidence to solve the woman's death.'

'Let me see this,' Olivia grabs the laptop from Harry, reading every detail, every word of the article. Without pictures of Sam in the article, she questions, 'It could have been another Sam Johnson? How do we know this is him?'

'How old is Sam now?'

'35.'

'This was ten years ago. It says in the article that this Sam Johnson was 25 when the girl died.'

'I don't believe it. I can't believe it. Even if it is the same Sam I know, I can't see him being involved in someone's death. He isn't a great guy, obviously, but he is no murderer.'

She looks over at Sam, her voice breaking with confusion and anger, 'Right, surely not?'

Harry attempts to remain calm, yet cautious of the situation, 'Please be careful, Liv, if it is the same guy, he was obviously a suspect for a reason, on top of that he is now stalking you and we really don't know what else he is capable of'?

More angst and confusion fill Olivia, 'I thought it was difficult enough finding out I am pregnant, without knowing all of this. Harry, what am I going to do?'

Needing to feel safe and supported, she pulls her chair closer to Harry and rests her head on his shoulders.

Chapter 16

Sam knows he shouldn't have got so angry and pushed Francesca but she infuriates him. The last place he wants to be is at home with her when she is demanding more from him. He watches as Francesca's cowardly runs upstairs after their altercation. He isn't going to chase after her.

He pours a last, final measure of whiskey, takes it over to the big sofa in the lounge, sits back and becomes fixated on a picture, a framed family photo taken a couple of years ago. The family were in Florida, the kids had just been to Disneyland, Nico and Bella were wearing Mickey Mouse ears with Francesca and Sam standing next to them, cuddling, laughing, happy. The photo is the epitome of a perfect family. Sam knows that, currently, this idea of them being a perfect family couldn't be further from the truth.

Nothing is as it seems, he thinks.

He stares at the photo, not recognising the person he was back then, for so many reasons he has changed. York has changed him; Olivia has changed him; all he wants is to be with her. Draining the last of the whisky from his glass he puts it back down on the table. There is the option to go upstairs and apologise to Francesca, even though he doesn't feel like this is his truth. Instead, he lies back on the sofa, fully clothed, throws the blanket over himself and closes his eyes. He wakes up the next morning to Nico tapping on his shoulder, wearing his navy spaceship pyjamas. 'Dad, what are you doing, why are you sleeping down here?'

A bleary-eyed Sam responds, 'Oh Nico, I must have fallen asleep watching TV. Have you seen your mum?'

'No, not yet' Nico responds.

'How are you feeling this morning, any better?'

'Not really.'

He demands, 'Go grab some cereal out of the cupboards, I am going to get your mum up, she will be down in a second.'

Sam walks up to the bedroom door, hand turning the bedroom handle. It is locked. He tries again, yanking it from side to side then knocking frantically.

'What do you want?' Francesca shouts from inside the bedroom.

'Let me in, I have to get ready for work, I am going to be late.'

Francesca walks towards the door, her hands shaking as she unlocks the door. As the door opens Sam races around the room, He does not look at her or take any interest, it is clear to Francesca that he feels no remorse or need to discuss the argument the night before. His attention and affection are no longer directed at Francesca, his thoughts and desires are held only for Olivia.

Sam demands, 'Nico is downstairs, wanting breakfast.'

A frustrated Francesca folds her arms and says, 'And you can't help, no?'

'Actually, I can't, I am already late for work so you are going to have to deal with it.'

Francesca shakes her head in disgust, walks out of the bedroom, heading downstairs.

Sam has an overwhelming feeling to want to escape his reality. For him, his reality is mundane. The excitement no longer comes from his wife, or kids, it comes from his intense affair with Olivia. He depends on her, to feel satisfied and whole.

But over the following weeks, there is a shift as Sam craves to be closer to her, she becomes more distant.

Feeling this distance between them, Sam questions Olivia about what has changed, but her response is cold and to the point. Showing no emotion and without detail or context, she communicates that she wants to remain as work colleagues. Hearing this, he can't help feeling confused and rejected.

Rejection was a prominent feeling throughout Sam's childhood, so as Olivia detaches from him, he is reminded of his past. His past is full of memories, a time where there was little love, affection shown. Growing up in a household where love was void has caused Sam to have deep rooted insecurities, needing reassurance and external attention, in order to feel seen and heard. Over time Sam has developed into someone with strong obsessive tendencies, where the feeling of being needed and loved was vital to his survival.

Without knowing it, he is now locked into a toxic cycle, where the more Olivia pulls away, the closer he wants to be. It has been a month since they have been intimate, but even with the passing of time, his need for her continues to grow, ruminating over every detail of their past love affair. Past fantasies and memories of their relationship plague his mind.

Slowly his insecurity creeps in and starts to dominate his thinking and actions. He starts to question if the reason they aren't together is because she has met someone else? Does she still think of him? He needs answers to these questions. So, after work and unknowing to Olivia he starts to follow her to see what intelligence he can gather to help him understand why she no longer wants to be with him, hoping the answer will put his mind to rest.

As the usual chaos unfolds in the Johnson household, a flustered Sam grabs the keys to Francesca's Mini and drives to work, late for the Tuesday weekly team meeting. As Robert chairs the meeting, talking through upcoming projects, Sam scans the room for the one face he desperately wants to see, Olivia, but she isn't in the meeting, where is she? He questions whether Olivia saw him outside her house last night. He needs to understand what she is doing and where she is.

After the meeting ends, Sam makes a coffee in the communal work kitchen, the hissing sound of the water boiling and people talking all around him add to his growing agitation. Acting on impulse and without saying a word he picks up his belongings and storms out of the door. He needs to see Olivia.

The Mini drives past The Walnut Garden and crawls past Olivia's house, he turns and parks enough distance to keep from being spotted by her but close enough to see the front door and her Blue Mercedes. Sam agonises over what to do next, whether he should knock on her front door or wait to see if she comes outside. There is no movement, nothing. Time passes. 11:20 am, 11:45 am, 12:15 pm, 12:40 pm, until suddenly there she is, leaving the house dressed in her joggers and sweatshirt. Her face is red and puffy as if she has been crying. Sam leans forward to capture her every movement. Olivia looks around, sees the Mini, without registering that it is Sam eagerly clutching the wheel, who is now slumped down in his seat so he can't be seen.

She darts her head around and proceeds to get into her car. Moments later the Mercedes wheels screech and race off. Sam follows. Speeding through the side roads, indicating, turning quickly, and frantically driving to the destination. Sam attempts to keep up with the car, without raising suspicion or getting noticed by Olivia. Reaching a junction, she turns right and before he can pull out two cars pass by in front of him. His face scrunches, knuckles punching the wheel, he is now three cars behind; he is about to lose her. Swerving left and right, attempting to get a better vision of the direction she is headed in, he sees her indicator, showing a left turn. Knowing he is back on her tail he sits back and relaxes a little into his chair. Olivia is only metres ahead of him now, down a residential road, so he breaks to create distance between the cars.

Olivia pulls over to park outside a terraced house. Sam slumps again in his seat as his car passes her. He notices a road on the right, so turns the car around ready to find a parking spot where he can park and watch the happenings unfold in the house. A location that is unknown to him. He reverses into a car space, close enough to see her car and the front door. A man with black curly hair and round glasses opens the door. Who is he? Is she already seeing somebody else, is that the reason for the distance? He questions everything?

Sam sits up quickly and watches as Olivia leaps forward and gives the mystery man a firm embrace. Jealousy and rage charge through Sam. He glares over, watching as they embrace for what feels like forever. Sam doesn't know what to think, he wants to scream, furious at what he is seeing. He can't make out what is being said before she heads inside and closes the door behind her.

He waits impatiently until finally, several hours later, she leaves the house. She is shaking her head, looking back at the figure in the doorway, words animated, obviously distressed. She heads back to her car, makes a U-turn, and sets off in the same direction she came. Sam allows her some space before turning on his engine and resumes following her. Thoughts stream through his consciousness.

What is he doing following Olivia, is he going to approach her when she arrives at her next destination, if so, what will he say? Sam doesn't know, all he knows is that he must talk to Olivia to find out everything.

Olivia's driving, once again erratic, weaves in and out of traffic, speeding, braking, the car jumping back and forward. Sam is two cars behind and sees the traffic lights up ahead turning a vibrant amber then red, Olivia accelerates just as the lights change to red.

'Shit!' Sam slams down the top of the wheel furiously, believing he has lost her in the car chase. He looks around at the surroundings, and notices he is now close to Olivia's home, a route he has taken countless times before. He is relieved to be back in control knowing that he will soon be able to confront her.

She gets out of her car, walks towards her house. Sam drives past and parks the car. He briskly walks over to Olivia's house. Just as Olivia is about to enter Sam shouts down the road, 'Liv!'

Her head turns anticipating the voice she now dreads to hear, eyes widening, she is terrified. 'What are you doing here? What do you want?'

'We need to talk, Liv,' Sam says approaching the gate.

'Not today, I have had a long day. I will call you tomorrow, OK?'

'No. This can't wait until tomorrow.'

Olivia is confused, 'What do you mean? What can't wait?'

'I have so many questions that need answering!' Sam disregards Olivia's plea and without another word he barges past into the house through the unlocked front door. Olivia stands on the doorstep frozen, witnessing the look of anger in Sam's eyes, not recognising the man in front of her. She wants to escape but instead her feet follow Sam into the house. She doesn't know what is about to happen, but she is on alert, fearful of what he could be capable off, especially after reading the article at Harry's.

Act calmly and don't mention the baby, she reminds herself.

Olivia closes the door; both are now standing in the dark hallway. Sam's shadow towers over Olivia, frightening her to the core. Hands shaking, unable to keep still, she turns the light on noticing the hardness and anger that is expressed all across his face. It takes all her power to calmly say, 'OK, let's go to the lounge and chat then.' Holding tightly onto her phone and car keys she walks past him into the lounge. Sam follows and yanks her forearm turning her around to face him and with an aggressive and loud tone he says, 'Where have you been today?'

Olivia tries to sound calm but instead her voice shakes, cracks under the immense pressure, 'I was with my best friend, you know Harry. I needed to talk to him about something.'

'Your ex Harry, about what?' Sam's face closing in, his grip still fixed tightly around her arm.

She responds quickly, 'About what? We were talking about work, my family. None of that really has anything to do with you.'

'Liar!' he yells.

'How long have you been seeing him, is that the reason you have been ignoring me? It is all starting to make sense now' Sam says grinding his teeth.

Olivia tries to remain composed, 'It's not like that.'

Underneath her calm exterior, she feels herself becoming flustered and angry. Angry at how foolish she was to be with this man and how her intuition could be so wrong.

Olivia doesn't know what to say. Before she knows it, six small words fall out of her mouth, blissfully unaware of the repercussions.

'You have obviously been hiding a lot from me…. I saw you in the paper!'

Sam releases the grip on Olivia's arm. His jaw tense, face turning a strong red colour. Closing in closer to her he scowls, 'What the hell did you just say?'

Olivia knows from his reaction that she has struck a nerve. Witnessing this reaction, she becomes aware that this man could definitely be the same Sam Johnson, once a suspect in a murder case. Instantly regretting the words but unable to stop, she continues anxiously, 'There was an article about a girl who died, and a Mr. Sam Johnson was named the key suspect.'

Olivia feels herself shrink in size under Sam's glare. He looks down at her, face growling, like an animal ready to pounce at its prey. Then in one quick sweep of violence, the vision in her right eye becomes dull, the room spinning quickly around her. She moves her head to try and touch her eyelid but before she does another violent blow is struck, this time catching the left side of her face, busting her lip open. She loses balance and falls backwards into the coffee table in the lounge. Olivia regains enough balance that she doesn't fall over completely. She puts her hands to her face, and then pulls away instantly as she feels the red, warm liquid cascade over her hands. With her vision still impaired, she can't see the blood that is pouring, she can only feel the warm sensation running down her face and into her mouth. Looking down to the carpet through her left eye, blood droplets plummet and soak into the beige carpet.

Olivia is in total disbelief, she tries to find the source of the wound and notices the right-hand side of her face has been cut open. Overcome by shock, she finally registers that she has been punched hard, twice. She feels scared, now scared for her life! Adrenaline ignites her survival mechanism, kicking her body into gear and suddenly fires chemicals around her body, giving her a rush of strength. Without a moment's hesitation and with newfound energy, she charges for the door at lightning speed, running past Sam and his beastly hands.

Still holding her car keys, she staggers onto the road, bewildered, embarrassed, and confused about what just happened. She opens her car door quickly and falls into the driver's seat, slamming the door, instantly locking it behind her.

Her face twitches, she checks the rear mirror to see that the left side of her face is swelling, eyes and lips are developing a strong marble of green and blue bruising. Starting the car engine, she accelerates at speed into the middle of the road and darts past her house. As soon as she is a safe distance, she looks back and sees the daunting silhouette of Sam overshadowing her doorway. His eyes glaring back. Olivia has now learnt that Sam is capable of stalking and assault. She is unsure of his next move and what he is truly capable of. She must go somewhere. Somewhere as far away from Sam as possible. Somewhere she can't be found, a place where she feels safe and protected.

Chapter 17

Sunlight streams brightly through the big window into Mr. Lint's therapy room. Lily pauses, takes a deep cleansing inhale, smelling the sweet tones of lavender that circle the room. Desperately searching for a moment of peace in the calm surroundings, but she can't. Instead, she feels uncomfortable, anxious.

'So let me just recap, you just said that being at the party that night took you further into a nightmare?' Mr. Lint gently probes for more details. 'What do you mean by that?'

Lily shakes her head, taking a while to respond. 'Well, the aftermath of the party sadly continued. A couple days later everybody that went to the party were called and interviewed by the police. We were informed that a girl had died that night. They interrogated us individually, asking if we knew who the girl was. If there were drugs at the party. If we had seen anything suspicious that night or have any information surrounding, what could have caused her death.'

Mr. Lint stays motionless, desperately quiet.

Lily's eyes begin to well-up. 'The next moment has played repeatedly in my mind, like a nightmare on repeat. On repeat for ten years. When the police interviewed me, I told them I didn't see anything or have any relevant information.'

The speed of her voice quickens, 'What you have to understand is that at the time I was very confused. I was on a terrible concoction of drugs and alcohol, so my perspective and emotions were all over the place. What I saw were two people having sex, I didn't know what was going on, naively believing that they could be a couple, just involved in some kinky play. I suppose I justified it to myself about what difference would it make if I said to the police that I saw two people having sex.'

'I can imagine you did what you thought was the right thing at the time?' Mr. Lint adds.

Lily continues, 'Yes. But you see, I then found out that a suspect was being charged for the case. I didn't know the suspect, but friends of Peter did, they showed me a picture of the guy. The worst part was he had the same hair and build as the man I saw having sex and there was another key factor. The guy in the picture had a birthmark on the side of his neck, the same mark i had seen on the man having sex at the party. The case never went to trial as there was not enough evidence to convict him. There were no witnesses.'

Mr. Lint says, 'So what are you saying?'

Lily fidgets in her chair, her voice louder and abrupt, 'I am saying that I think I was potentially a witness to a murder and didn't disclose the information to the police!'

A baffled Mr. Lint speaks slowly and compassionately, 'Oh, I see.'

'Believe me this has eaten me up ever since. I have flashbacks of that night, about the noises I heard, the figures I saw in the bedroom. I rack my brain to see, if I looked deeper into my memory, would I be able to piece anymore information together. I know I have to try and move on, but I feel so guilty. I should have just come forward and given the evidence I had at the time.'

'What was the name of the suspect?' Mr. Lint asked.

'Sam Johnson!' Lily exclaims.

By telling Mr. Lint this story, Lily feels lighter and free, it is as if a huge mental weight has been lifted from her shoulders. This is the story she has been scared to tell anyone but now, having done so, she feels more confident to face her past and demons.

Chapter 18

Blood drips from his ghastly hands. Sam is furious, eyebrows furrowed, heart racing. How could Olivia mention a case buried so deep in the past? Sam thinks. It has been ten years since the night of the party, but the repercussions still continue to haunt him.

He moved his family out of London wanting to create more distance from the murder case and everything that surrounded that night. Whenever he was back in his hometown, he felt surrounded by fear and paranoia that people were whispering, staring, glaring at him, knowing what he has done.

He hoped York would be a new start but now the one person that Sam felt comfortable with, is the same person that has uncovered his darkest secret.

In a fit of complete rage, he lunged at Olivia, and delivered two swift punches. He looks down to his bruised and bloody knuckles that are pulsing, aching from the blows. As he inspects his hands, salty sweat pours from his forehead, his breathing is erratic. He stands frozen, uncertain of what to do next.

In his confused state, he is unaware of Olivia running past him, darting out of the door. As soon as he realises, he walks out of the front door to see the Mercedes screeching down the road so quickly that the vehicle leaves a burning smell of rubber. Trying to gather his composure, he wanders into the downstairs bathroom, turns on the tap and watches the water as it streams over his knuckles that are split open. The shock of the water seeping into his deep cuts makes him gasp. Hands shaking under the tap, the clear water has turned a deep maroon colour which then fades into a light pink. Sam looks up at himself in the mirror, eyes glazed, cheeks red, face full of anger and adrenalin. He turns the tap off and leans his tense, tight body over the sink. He picks up the white Egyptian cotton hand towel and pats his face to cool down, then wipes the remaining dried blood off his hands.

What does he do next? He thinks over and over. He cleans himself, making sure he looks presentable not wanting to arouse suspicion to Francesca or anyone else.

Sam leaves Olivia's house, he quickly gets back into the car and drives home. Over the next couple of days, he blocks the assault out of his mind, resumes his daily life route, attempting to bring a sense of normality back into to his life. As much as he tries to hide the altercation there is still the physical reminder, the trace of a deep wound set into his knuckles.

Olivia has now been out of the office for a couple of days, with no communication, causing her colleagues to stir and question her whereabouts. As Sam arrives at the office on Thursday, expecting a normal day, he is immediately approached by Robert who is tense and noticeably irritable. He storms over to Sam, questioning him about Olivia.

He hardly takes a breath as he blurts out, 'Hi, Sam, have you heard anything from Olivia, nobody can get through to her? It has been a couple of days since her text on Tuesday morning, do you know anything? It is not like her to not phone or let me know that she is OK. Have you spoken to her?'

'No. I haven't been in touch with her, is everything OK?'

'This is so not like Olivia. I mean where could she be?'

Sam tries to sound empathetic and reassuring, 'I wish I knew, Robert. I don't know what to tell you.'

'OK. If I hear anything, I will let you know, I know you and Olivia have become close since working together.'

'Thanks,' Sam responds.

'Are you able to handle the Isla Bourne scheme on your own in the meantime? If not, I can get someone else to work on it with you.'

'Don't worry about that, you can trust me. I will deal with it Hopefully Olivia will be back soon to pick the work up.'

'I do hope so. Thanks, Sam, I appreciate it. If you need anything, let me know.' Robert attempts a small smile masking over his distress.

Watching Robert walking away, Sam immediately becomes engulfed in paranoia. He needs space to calculate a response if he is faced with more questioning, so he heads to the small, independent coffee shop, Coffee Makers. He sits in the window, sipping on a double shot latte. Feeling conflicted, he is missing Olivia. Missing everything about her, but he knows he must switch off any emotions and feel more in control.

As he walks back into the office this feeling of control is instantly depleted when suddenly out of the corner of his eye, he sees two figures of authority with Robert in the conference room. Sam's beady eyes stare at them all, suspicious of their conversation. A stern Robert notices Sam and points over in his direction. The two police officers turn their gaze and are now directing their attention towards him.

Robert opens the conference room door, 'Sam, have you got a minute, would you mind popping in here, we need a chat.' Sam doesn't reply, he just nods and walks sheepishly into the conference room, not making eye contact with the police officers. He takes a quick moment to think strategically on the best approach, puffs out his chest and turns on any remaining charm that is left within him.

Sam is fearful of what happens next but manages to greet the two police officers with a false, warm tone, 'Morning.' A woman and male stare back at him, blankly. The man is short but built with a shaved head, the woman is pretty, her hair pulled back into a tight ponytail.

'The police would like to ask you a couple of questions about Olivia if that's OK?' Robert sits down at the conference table and everyone else follows.

Sam takes a seat, putting his hands intertwined on the boardroom table. He quickly notices his swollen knuckles, so without hesitation and before anyone notices, he subtly takes them off the table and places them in his lap. Hiding evidence out of plain sight.

'Mr. Johnson, I am DC Clark, this is DC Edwards,' the woman states. 'We have a growing concern from Mr. Brindles as to the whereabouts of Olivia Bloom. The last known communication was a text on Tuesday morning to say that she wasn't feeling well and wouldn't be in the office. Robert and colleagues have had not heard from her since then and I believe that, for Olivia, this is unusual, out of character behaviour. We went over to her home address yesterday to see if she was there but she doesn't seem to be currently home and her car has gone. We have also contacted her parents last night but they have not heard from her for several days. As it has been over 24 hrs that anyone has been in contact with her, Olivia is now classed as a missing person.'

'We need to ask some questions from those immediately around her to gain any intelligence as to where she might be or could have gone.'

'I totally understand; whatever you need. I promise to help where I can.' Sam tries to focus on staying relaxed.

'I believe you are relatively new to the firm, how are you finding it?'

'The team are great, the job is fulfilling, I can't complain.'

'That's good to hear, I understand you were working on a relatively new project with Olivia?'

'Yes, that's correct.'

'How is the project going?'

'It's not been long since I first met Olivia, about two months, but we won the new project, I think we make a great team.'

Sam continues to talk softly and slowly, appearing to be at ease with the further questioning, 'I think Robert could see from the start there would be a synergy between us, and I suppose that was the reason we were assigned to work on the development in the first place.'

'And when did you last see her?'

As Sam's mind scans back to when he had last seen her, his senses become hyper focused, the office lights seem to be unusually bright and he is overtly aware of the heat from the lights beating down on his face, hands becoming warm, mouth feeling dry and dehydrated.

It is a couple of days since Sam and Olivia had the altercation at her house, but he isn't going to mention that. He finally responds, trying to sound confident, 'The beginning of the week when she was last in the office.'

'So what day was that exactly?' The DC continues.

Sam does not appreciate the questioning, are they accusing him of something, he thinks?

He tries to hide his irritation and stays composed replying, 'Monday.'

'How did she seem when you saw her on Monday then, anything out of the ordinary, unusual?'

'Same as she always is, I suppose. Relaxed, professional. Nothing out of the ordinary. We were busy discussing the scheme. She didn't mention anything that would have alarmed me in anyway.'

'Have you seen her or been in touch since Monday?'

Sam is aware of the direct and personal nature of the questions, shifts slightly in the chair and responds immediately, 'No. Nothing.'

DC Edwards looks intently at Sam and advises, 'If you hear anything from Olivia or have any more information, please get in touch as soon as possible. The next couple of days are critical in our search and the safety of Miss Bloom.'

DC Clark and DC Edwards look back at Robert, nod and without saying a word they stand up.

Robert also stands up and says, 'Thanks, I will see you out. 'DC Clark responds with, 'Thanks for your time, have a good day.'

Sam watches as the police officers leave, letting out a long anxious sigh.

Chapter 19

Bloodied hands hold the steering wheel, legs shaking as she presses firmly onto the accelerator. Her right eye is swelling, closing shut with the occasional drip of blood onto her sweatshirt. At a red light, she searches the glove compartment for a tissue and gently holds it to her eye, shock running throughout her body as she lightly dabs the wound. Nervously checking the mirror to see if she is being followed but thankfully, Sam is nowhere to be seen. On auto pilot, Olivia heads for the A1. With every mile further away from York, she feels closer to safety, heading south towards her family home in East Sussex, Olivia switches off her phone, wanting to isolate herself from her desperate reality.

As the night gets darker, Olivia stops only for fuel at a service station. She takes the M25 then the M23, the last leg of the journey, at last reaching her destination. The journey has taken nearly five hours. She looks at the clock on the dashboard; the time reads 9:50 pm.

Pulling into the driveway of her parent's farmhouse, the road forks right to the main house and left to the guest cottage. She turns left, embarrassed, not wanting her parents to see her this way; she doesn't have the energy to explain what happened, not tonight and maybe not tomorrow. Olivia needs time on her own to digest all the information. No lights are on in the farmhouse; feeling relieved that her parents must not be at home. Olivia parks behind the cottage; her car unseen from the main house, gets out and heads towards the front door. She bends over and lifts a flowerpot to find the key underneath. She picks up the key and opens the door to the cottage, a small self-contained house. As the front door shuts, she falls back and cries, breathing a sigh of relief that she is away from the chaos outside, allowing herself to emotionally let go. As the adrenaline slowly expels from her body it leaves an underlying throbbing pain. Feeling the sensation, she weeps then suddenly screams in the empty house, releasing her deep, raging, frustration and hurt.

Completely exhausted, emotionally and physically she makes her way up the stairs towards the bedroom. She collapses onto the bed fully clothed, moving from side to side, trying to get comfortable. She closes her eyes, only waking up to Larry, her parent's cockerel, crowing early the following day. She is relieved hearing this noise, a familiar, comforting sound from her past.

It doesn't take long before recollections of the event yesterday haunt her. She inhales sharply and closes her eyes, still exhausted, quickly falling back to sleep, her body and mind are now out of "*danger*" and in recovery mode.

Olivia spends the day, falling in and out of sleep, consciously aware of the pain that has been inflicted on her body.

Eventually when she does manage to stagger to the bathroom, she notices her reflection. Shocked, at the face that is staring back at her. Her face is unrecognisable, there is a large black and blue bruise that covers her right eye and across half her face, the bridge of her nose and lips are swollen. Olivia is haunted by the horror of yesterday which is now physically visible for all to see.

She recalls the look of rage on Sam's face, his aggressive, violent nature, his fist flying towards her face. Tears begin to stream down her face. Olivia is a strong woman who never imagined she would be in this position. Never thinking she would be someone who would hide in the shadows. She allows herself to feel all the emotions deep in her stomach, the process of letting go makes her feel physically sick. She retches and retches again, grasping onto the bathroom sink, steadying herself as she violently throws up.

Head pounding, she slips back under the sheets, remembering a happier time, a time before Sam Johnson. A life filled with abundant success, recognition at work, inner self confidence. Olivia craves to reconnect with her old self. It is only when she reflects that she realises she has lost some of herself, her identity. But for right now, her focus is how to navigate the abuse and pain afflicted upon her. She wants to hide away from the outside world and the truth, at least for a while.

Olivia wakes up in the early morning light. It has been a day and a half of not seeing anyone, keeping herself isolated; all this time disconnected from the world, keeping her phone off, needing time to process and think about what to do next, what to do about work. Does she tell Robert about what happened? Or the police? What about the baby, does she keep it?

Turning her phone on, notifications immediately flash on the screen. There are several messages from Robert, asking if she is feeling better and when she will be back in the office.

There are text messages and missed calls from her parents, sounding extremely concerned, they have mentioned that the police have been in touch. Olivia's anxiety levels rise significantly when she sees a bombardment of missed calls from Sam. Knowing that he has tried to call is overwhelming and suffocating.

Her brief period of isolation allows Olivia to gather her strength, now determined that Sam will face the consequences of his actions. She puts back on her blood stained and nervously calls her parents. They answer immediately and begin to question Olivia. She reassures them that everything is OK, attempting to keep them calm, and mentions she has been staying in their cottage.

Olivia spends time composing herself, prepared to drive the short journey from the cottage to the main house and explain everything. Approaching the farmhouse, she is bombarded with thoughts about what will happen next and her parent's reaction. Her car crunches over the small, gravel stones on the drive and stops outside the house.

Before Olivia can ring the bell the door swings open. Her parents stand their looking alarmed, gasping at their daughter's appearance. Their shattered hearts are slightly tempered by relief that their daughter is no longer missing. Throughout Olivia's childhood, her parents did everything they could to protect her, keep her safe. Her happiness has always been the most important thing to them. Her mum grabs Olivia and pulls her close for a warm, loving embrace, wanting to take away any of the pain. Her father, looks on, walks towards them and puts his protective wide arms around both, sheltering them. The family stand there for a long moment, silently, just affectionately holding each other.

The tight embrace is broken by Olivia's mum as she wipes a tear from her eye. Her dad puts his arms around her shoulder as they shuffle towards the kitchen. He goes over to the kettle to make some tea while Olivia and her mum sit down at the large kitchen table.

Olivia knows she needs to find the strength to relive and explain everything that has happened over the last two months. Hesitantly, she starts at the beginning, talking about how she met Sam, how guilty she felt knowing that he is married with kids. How this went against her moral compass but she submerged this feeling due to the deep sense of connection she felt. Her parents sit at the table supportive, listening without judgement, not wanting to add their opinions to an already complicated situation.

Olivia confides in her parents about the stalking, the article sharing details of Sam's past, the assault and the unplanned pregnancy. Throughout the conversation, she feels moments of great anger that shift to deep vulnerability and sadness. Olivia feels lost within her own story, as if the situation, trauma belongs to someone else. Her parents sit back in their chairs, faces in dismay, heads shaking, eyes glazed over, they never said a word until the end.

'Your mum and I have been so worried about you. We are just so glad you are home safe. You have been through a lot, and we are so sorry. The police have been in touch, asking if we knew where you were. I think the first thing we need to do is call them and for you to tell your story. He can't get away with this,' her dad blurts out.

Olivia anxiously plays with her nails, she takes a while to respond, 'I know I do, but please not today. I don't have the strength and just want to spend some time with you both. I need to re-gather my strength, physically and psychologically, before I explain the situation all over again. I really don't have the energy right now.'

Dad reassuringly nods and replies, 'OK, let's talk to them first thing tomorrow. Your mum and I will be with you, right by your side.' Olivia looks back and gives a grateful smile in acknowledgement.

Her dad continues calmly, 'Also Olivia what are your thoughts about the baby? Are you going to keep it?'

Her mum interrupts empathetically, 'Whatever you choose to do honey, we will support you, no matter what. Let me make some brunch, you must be starving. How about your favourite, pancakes with bacon?' Olivia smiles, sinking further back into her chair, feeling surrounded by love. She begins to eat and starts to think of her life she has ran away from in York and if it will ever be the same again? She looks at her phone and realises it is Thursday afternoon. Usually, on a Thursday she would be on a site visit. How quickly life can change in only a few days, she ponders.

Suddenly Olivia says, 'I have decided. I am going to have this baby. I know it is not going to be easy, given the circumstances.'

Her dad looks on in surprise.

Olivia, noticing the reaction, begins to explain, 'Being a mum has always been part of my life plan. I know the way it has all happened is far from ideal but at the end of the day, this is still my baby.' Her voice breaks. 'I have people around me that love me and will be there to support, love us both.'

Her mum places her hand on top of Olivia's, 'Your baby will have all our love.' She reaches over to hug Olivia in her chair, eyes welling with emotion. 'You will be the best mum; I just know it.'

Chapter 20

Lily's Friday continues as normal, spending a couple of hours before work drinking coffee, shopping online and looking at BBC World News to keep up to date with current affairs. Understanding what is going on in the UK and the wider world makes her feel less isolated in Australia. Reading the news articles reignites her passion for journalism, seeing how journalists collect, prepare and broadcast stories for public consumption. Mr. Lint and Charlie have been instrumental in rebuilding her confidence and now, more than ever, she begins to visualise herself there on the screen reporting and commentating on events.

The mouse scrolls through the latest bulletins, eyes darting around her laptop, reading the online articles when her attention is drawn by a picture of a beautiful woman with long, dark curly hair and the headline: "Missing. A woman has gone missing in York." Lily feels instantly connected to this article. The woman pictured can't be much older than Lily, she wants to know more. Who is this woman? What is she like? Why is she missing? So many questions, the aspiring journalist within Lily begins to creep out.

The article states: "Olivia Bloom, a top architect working at New Dawn Architects in York, is now reported missing."

Reading the details, Lily's world drastically changes. An article that just held a small level of intrigue and mystery suddenly becomes real. Two words she had spent ten years trying to forget jumps from the page into her consciousness: Sam Johnson! There is a quote from a man called, Sam Johnson which reads, 'Olivia is not only a very talented architect but a kind friend.'

Lily's mind begins to spiral into thought, surely it isn't the same Sam Johnson that was involved in the Box Hill case? It is a fairly common name but please let it be another Sam Johnson, she thinks. Her inquisitive nature compels her to seek further information. Crouching over her laptop, banging on the keyboards, new tab, search, mind racing a hundred miles an hour, she punches in New Dawn Architects into Google and finds a press announcement in the Architects' Journal:

Robert Brindles, Managing Director from New Dawn Architects quotes, 'Here at New Dawn we have been fortunate to win some of the biggest commercial developments in Yorkshire. To support the expansion and wins within our portfolio we are excited to welcome Sam Johnson. Sam is an award-winning architect who brings his skills and knowledge to our ever-growing team. His recent involvement and leadership at the Embankment project in London impressed us, and we are very excited that he has decided to move to New Dawn.' Next to the press release is a small photograph showing Sam in a grey suit. There is he, the man of her nightmares, with his smug face and false smile, brown hair but, most of all, the distinctive birth mark on the side of his neck. This is a face that she recalls all too well.

Lily stares at the photograph in disbelief. The fear, heart racing, adrenalin fires fiercely through her body. She becomes terrified, feeling as if she is back at the house party all those years ago. She is struggling to tell the difference between her thoughts and reality. Flashbacks of Sam with his strong hands around the girl's neck overrides her thinking.

Her focus then turns to Olivia Bloom and where she could be and if she is safe? Intuition tells Lily that Sam Johnson could be involved with this woman's disappearance and if he is involved, she didn't even want to think of the possible consequences.

Lily looks at her watch; it's time to get ready for work. That evening, as she worked her shift, it seemed like an out of body experience as if she was watching herself serve drinks and chat mindlessly to the customers, truly not engaged in the conversation. Her mind was elsewhere, she could not stop thinking about Olivia Bloom and what she should do.

Although Lily has no insight about the disappearance of Olivia Bloom, she does have knowledge of the events surrounding the Box Hill murder, the same man that is mentioned in the article. There may be no correlation and Sam Johnson may be a totally innocent party in the Olivia Bloom case but her gut feeling, and the coincidence of it all plays on Lily's mind.

She is torn about whether to come forward to the police to tell them the story she has kept buried for so long. There is the option to not say anything and live the life she has been living, but that means continuing to carry a heavy burden.

Lily has struggled tremendously over the last ten years, her mother's death, looking after her dad and brother, as well as trying to find her direction and purpose in life. Lily believed travelling the world would help her escape her past but now the nightmare of that night at the party has never felt closer.

Lily realises, this is it, the time to face her fears. She will no longer hide from the questions that have tortured her. With the help of Mr. Lint and the joy of the relationship with Charlie, she is determined to stop worrying about the consequences and do the right thing.

She decides to call North Yorkshire Police. She leaves her shift at 12.30am on Saturday morning and after checking the time difference sees it is 1.30pm on Friday afternoon in the UK. She searches the number then slowly pushes the buttons on her phone, tapping in the dialling code. *Breathe, Lily, you have got this, you are doing the right thing*, she thinks trying to convince herself.

Chapter 21

There is high energy in the North Yorkshire Police Headquarters late on Thursday evening. The station is filled with the palpable energy of officers talking loudly, impatiently on the phone, the meeting rooms are filled with boards, marker pens, TV screens and images that are connected to different cases. The atmosphere is electric, tension all around.

There have been no warm leads surrounding the whereabouts of Olivia Bloom. The woman is reported as last seen in the office on Monday. DC Clark understands how critical the first week is to solve a missing person case, so they frantically work against the clock, gathering evidence and trying to uncover any motive. But to their dismay nothing suspicious has arisen from the interviews with her work colleagues, family and friends surrounding her whereabouts.

DC Clark needs to now generate public awareness about Olivia Bloom and the case. With a sense of urgency in her tone, she shouts over to DC Edwards, 'It's time to ramp up the search. Can you speak to DC Sand and push the button on the missing persons' article; we need to reach as many other people as soon as we possibly can.' DC Edwards walks over to DC Sand, looks at his computer screen, begins to point and talk quickly. He walks back to DC Clark. 'It's done, it will be released across publications, immediately.'

'Thanks, Edwards, let's hope the release generates some leads. Sadly, as it stands, we have garnered very little information.'

DC Edwards folds his arms, nods, listening to DC Clark as she continues, 'It is high priority that we gather any intelligence we can. At this point I will action the necessary means to carry out a full forensic search of her house.'

She looks down at her watch, 'It will more than likely be tomorrow afternoon, if you can meet the forensic investigators at her address, that would be much appreciated.'

Olivia is safe in her hideaway, unaware of the developments that have unfolded through the night. A loud knock pounds on Olivia's bedroom door, startling and waking her up. She awakens to see her mum and dad distressed, they rush in and dramatically sit themselves down on her bed.

'Sorry to alarm you honey but we have some news. It seems that you are in the paper.'

Olivia bolts up, sitting straight in bed. 'What do you mean, I am in the paper?'

Her mum continues, 'When the police rang us two days ago, we had no idea where you were, we told them that we couldn't get through to you. As we didn't go to the station yesterday and you were last reported seen in the office on Monday, they posted an article in the York Press that has been picked up by other media outlets. They have raised the alarm and want to talk to any witnesses that may have seen you.'

Olivia reaches over to grab her phone and sees her face plastered all over the internet, a narrative about a missing woman from York. How did it get to this? She switches off her emotions and taps into her practical side. The articles give her the urgency to come forward to the police and give her statement, version of the events that have unfolded.

The reality that has unfolded around Olivia seems to be surreal. With her mind racing with so many unanswered questions, the family drive the 45 minutes to Sussex police headquarters. Olivia sits in the police reception, feeling safe, surrounded by love and support. 'Miss Bloom?' a male office shouts looking up from a notepad. She nods and follows him into a small room at the side of reception. Before she walks through the door, she looks back at her parents; they nod back in encouragement as she proceeds into the room. She gives her statement and walks back out of the room after 1 pm, Friday afternoon.

As soon as she leaves the station, East Sussex police immediately phone the lead officer on the case in York, DC Clark, relaying the information that Olivia has just disclosed.

Chapter 22

The press release of Olivia has generated awareness, interest and the desired result, East Sussex police have called to advise that Olivia is now safe. Her statement is a full disclosure, highlighting information about the affair and the attack from Mr. Johnson.

With this knowledge, DC Clark scribbles down key notes from the call and fills out the necessary paperwork to arrest Mr. Johnson and bring him in for questioning.

No sooner has DC Clark finished writing the notes, the phone rings again. This time a call has been transferred over from reception.

'North Yorkshire police, DC Clark, how can I help?'

A woman's voice on the phone sounds shaky and nervous. 'Hi, I need to speak to someone; I am a witness to a case.'

'OK, which case are you referring to?'

'The Box Hill house party murder.'

'Box Hill? I am sorry that does not ring a bell. Can you provide further information Miss?'

'Well, the party was ten years ago.'

DC Clark is surprised and perplexed as to why the call has been forwarded on to her. Knowing that she needs to immediately leave the station and arrest Sam Johnson, she thinks of cutting the conversation short.

'Ten years?' DC Clark says with a sense of irritation.

'Yes, I am calling as I think it might be relevant for the recent missing woman case in York, you know Olivia Bloom.'

'Oh, I see. I am the lead detective on that case. Can I start by taking your name please?'

Lily becomes increasingly nervous, she stutters. 'Yes, it's Lily, Lily Hayes.'

DC Clark grabs her notebook and pen.

'OK, great. So how do you know Olivia?'

'I don't know Olivia or live in York but have some evidence that may lead to finding out where she could be. You see the guy mentioned in the article, Sam Johnson, I know him. Well, I don't really know him but I was a witness to a previous case where he was the key suspect.'

'Sorry, I am not following,' DC Clark announces, trying to piece together the significance of what the woman is saying.

Lily stumbles over the first couple of words, 'OK. Let me start again.' Lily pauses, takes a deep breath and continues, this time speaking more eloquently. 'Sam Johnson was a key suspect in 2012 for the murder of a woman. He was never convicted because there wasn't enough evidence against him. I don't really know how to say this, so I am just going to confess that I was a witness to the event. As hazy as my memory is, I saw him and the girl that died…they were together before she died.'

'Just so I am clear you are saying that you were a witness to a murder ten years ago and never came forward.'

'That's right, I never came forward. I don't really want to go into the reason why I didn't, that's a long story.' Lily then begins to brief DC Clark about that night, what she had seen and heard.

'I am not saying he is involved with Olivia Bloom's disappearance but ever since that night at Box Hill, keeping this information secret has eaten me alive. From what I saw I am coming forward now as I wanted to give you the full picture of what this man could be capable of, in the event that it may be helpful, that is all.'

'Thanks, Miss Hayes, we appreciate you disclosing this information. You have done the right thing.'

Lily enquires, 'I mean this case happened ten years ago, can he be put on trial after all this time?'

'Yes, Lily. Yes, he can.'

DC Clarks hears a sharp inhale down the end of the phone, she knows this is not the answer Lily expects so softens her tone. 'Lily, as it stands, he was charged but the case never went to trial. What you have just told me is classed as new evidence which strongly links him to the woman's death at that party. I know you are living in Australia, but it is paramount you make a full statement and when this goes to trial, because it will from what you have told me, that you are here to testify on the stand against him. As you said, we do not know what he is capable of but if it turns out that he is a threat to society, we must act and do all we can, so this never happens to anyone else, another victim. Do you understand?'

Lily remains silent, speechless. This is an unexpected turn of events, one which Lily never saw happening.

DC Clark continues in a gentle manner attempting to get Lily to cooperate, 'I can appreciate this is probably a lot of new information to take in, why don't you think about it and call me when you want to do the statement, I will give you my direct line. Does that sound OK to you?'

DC Clark gives her number to Lily. Lily knows she must give her statement and make up for the wrong she has felt she has done in the past.

She puts the phone down and pushes her shoulder length hair behind her ears, standing and looking over at her investigative assistant, DC Sand who is typing away on his keyboard at the desk opposite.

'OK listen up, we have yet another development in the case! Olivia Bloom has given a statement, the details of which are enough evidence to detain Mr. Johnson. As if this day couldn't get any crazier, there is more news.'

'What do you mean, more?' DC Sand responds.

'Well, I just spoke to a witness to a murder ten years ago, it is the first time she has come forward to testify.'

'And?' DC Sand asks.

'The witness saw Mr. Johnson with the woman that died, Abigail West. Her statement incriminates him in Abigail's death. So, we need to act quickly. In terms of next steps, can you contact the Surrey Police, update them on the findings today and find out all you can about that case, every detail? I want the witness interviews from that time as well as any forensic findings.'

DC Clark's voice now picks up speed. 'DC Edwards is at Olivia Bloom's house with the forensics team. I am going to give him a call to update. I need to pick him up as soon as possible and then head over to Mr. Johnson's house. We can potentially charge him on two counts, one for the murder of Abigail West and the second of aggravated assault to Olivia

Bloom. This man is now a threat to public safety and with the serious offences we have been informed of, there is enough evidence to detain him in custody until the date of the trial.'

Chapter 23

The residential street is quiet, birds sing softly from the heights of great oak trees that line the road. DC Edwards is parked outside Olivia's house. There is another car behind that belongs to the Crime Scene Investigator and Forensic Scientists. DC Edwards stands at the front door, grabs his latex gloves and feet coverings and moves aside to allow the forensic investigator to wipe down the door handle and the area around the key lock, with the aim to pick up any fingerprints.

The CSI and Forensic Investigator then cover Olivia's door with crime scene barricade tape, securing and protecting the house. DC Edwards calls over to them, 'Let's see what we can find.' What was once Olivia's haven is now a crime scene.

Before DC Edwards has a chance to step into the house his phone vibrates, taking off his gloves off to see that DC Clark is calling.

'Edwards, there is news, two big developments. East Sussex police have called, they have Olivia Bloom, and it seems Sam Johnson assaulted her on Tuesday afternoon. Not only that, we have a recent report that he is connected to a separate murder case in Surrey. I'll explain the details when I see you. Collect what evidence you can at the scene, I am coming to pick you up in 20 minutes, we are then heading straight over to Mr. Johnson's house to detain him. If he isn't there, we will go to the New Dawn office. We need to find and arrest him, today.'

"All understood" DC Edwards replies as he looks at his watch. He follows the CSI and forensic investigator into the house. Walking around the house, he notices a family portrait. In the picture, Olivia is stood between two older people, hugging them tightly. They are all beaming with happiness. The love and affection in the picture is clear to see; he expects that the two people are Olivia's parents. In the background of the picture, there is a row of white cliffs on the edge of a beach. Edwards shouts over to the CSI who is surveying the hall, 'Come take a look at this, where is this photo taken?'

The CSI responds, 'That looks to be the Seven Sisters?'

'Seven Sisters?'

'You know the white cliffs on the channel.'

DC Edwards says, 'That makes sense, Olivia's parents are from East Sussex.'

'Edwards, we have found something,' calls one of the forensic investigators from the downstairs bathroom, his direct voice can be heard from the lounge. He immediately walks over.

'There are traces of blood on this hand towel; we will send it for analysis to see if it is of value.'

DC Edwards questions, 'Do you believe that an altercation took place? Is there any other evidence to suggest that an intruder was in the house?'

The forensic investigator places the towel into a small see-through bag, then points to the coffee table which is positioned at a strange angle in the centre of the room. He moves the coffee table to show DC Edwards what appears to be blood stains near the table base, the blood droplets have soaked and created small circles on the cream carpet, turning the fabric a dark maroon colour. Suddenly bright lights flash and bounce off the walls, clicking sounds can be heard as the forensic investigator takes pictures of the carpet stains.

The investigator continues, 'DC Edwards there is sufficient evidence to suggest that there has been a conflict in the house.'

'Good work. Let's get this evidence over to the lab as quickly as possible to run the DNA and fingerprints.'

Chapter 24

Sam lies in bed, irritated and frustrated thinking about yesterday. What should have been a normal Thursday in the office was disrupted by a police interview. Were they interrogating him? Do they know something? His mind spiralling out of control.

He looks at his phone, it is 7:30 am, the familiar sounds can be heard outside of his bedroom, kids running around getting ready for school, cereal bowls clanking on the kitchen table and Francesca calling after them, attempting to get them ready for school. He puts the pillow over his head trying to hide from reality and sleep for a little longer but with all the surrounding chaos he picks up his phone, glances over Architects Journal and the BBC News. There he sees the article and recognises that beaming, bright smile, a picture of Olivia Bloom with big, bold italics that scream across the page, "Missing."

His heart thuds quicker and quicker, tunnel vision focusing on the article, the real world around him now seems blurry and distant. He reads the headline: '30-year-old Olivia Bloom is reported missing. If anyone has any information of her whereabouts, please come forward and call the police immediately.'

Sam wants nothing more than to see Olivia again and go back to being together, but he reluctantly knows that it is too late! The thought of being without her is devastating, he is so enveloped in his own thoughts that he struggles to connect, think of anything outside of his past life with Olivia.

The idea of small talk with his colleagues about the recent article fills him with dread. He can't face the real world, not today. The only reasonable solution is to separate from any distraction and work from home.

Sam attempts to resume normality and work but his mind is paralysed with fear and anxiety, questioning Olivia's whereabouts and if she is planning to come forward about the attack.

As Francesca potters around the kitchen, she is blissfully unaware of what is unfolding around her, remaining oblivious to Sam and his inner nightmare. Nico and Bella have half a day at school on a Friday so Sam manages to find a brief moment of silence when Francesca picks them up, to his dismay the noise quickly resumes as the family re-enter the house.

Nico and Bella with beaming smiles, excitedly run towards Sam working on the kitchen table. He gives them both a warm embrace. The children have the ability to settle his anxiety. He lets them go, looks deep into their eyes, and feels a short burst of relief. For a fleeting moment, they take some of his stress and anguish away and remind him of a place where Olivia isn't the centre of his world.

But that moment of pause is quickly overshadowed by his incessant need to refresh the news on his phone, seeking any updates. It is all becoming too much. Thoughts about Olivia, where she is? What will happen? Needing his mind to stop the inner torment, desperately wanting a distraction he storms into the fridge and grabs a beer from the fridge, guzzling the crisp, cold beverage.

The distraction is short lived, fleeting and no sooner does Sam find himself back in reality. Staring blankly at the now empty bottle he is startled by a large, intimidating knock that angrily bangs on the front door. Sam stays fixed, frozen and listens intently as Francesca opens the front door, his ears hyper focused, analysing the muffled noises that are now vibrating through the walls.

Francesca storms into the kitchen, fear, and confusion evident on her face. She abruptly questions, 'What the hell is going on?'

She looks down at her hands that are shaking and continues, 'The police are here wanting to talk to you about something? They said that it is urgent.'

Sam forcefully slams the bottle onto the table, puffs out his chest and replies, 'What are you talking about? Why?'

Francesca's fights her anxiety and replies, 'I don't know Sam.'

He marches over to the door to see two officers glaring directly at him, they are the same police officers that lead the uncomfortable interrogation in the office. Their faces are illuminated by the flashing lights on the police car behind them.

'Mr Johnson?' the female officer asks.

Sam, shocked and speechless, remains silent as DC Clark continues, 'You are under arrest on suspicion of murder. The murder of Miss. Abigail West and aggravated assault against Olivia Bloom. You do not have to say anything, but it may harm your defence if you do not mention, when questioned something which you later rely on in court. Anything you do say may be given in evidence.'

Sam is still motionless, eyes wide staring at the police. He replays the officer's statement in his mind, *Abigail West,* he thinks. That is a name he has not heard in ten years.

Becoming uneasy and irritable he shouts, 'Abigail West? What? I don't understand!'

'Yes. All will be revealed when we get to the station but we have received evidence that connects YOU to her death!' With a tight grip on Sam's shoulders, DC Clark turns him around. Sam hears the rattling, clinking noise from the handcuffs before they trap his wrists together.

Francesca watches on as her husband is arrested. With a spiralling number of questions, she shouts furiously at Sam, 'What is going on? Who is Abigail West? Murder? And Olivia Bloom isn't that the woman you work with. Sam, tell me what is going on?'

Sam's eyes glaze over, staring at her vacantly.

Nico and Bella don't understand the commotion as they run up to Francesca and pull on her jumper asking with great concern and sadness, 'Mummy, Mummy, what is going on?'

Sam, looks down to them and in a cold tone exclaims, 'I have done nothing!' His voice is loud and aggressive. He sees Nico and Bella, their eyes welling up with terror and emotion. Tears fall uncontrollably down their reddened cheeks.

Sam notices their pain and feels a sharp burst of tightness across his chest as DC Clark pulls on the handcuffs directing Sam towards the police car. With one hand she places her palm onto his head and eases Sam into the back of the police car.

Sam looks out of the window to see the family he has now left behind. Francesca, Nico and Bella all stare as the police car door shuts behind Sam, locking him in the backseat. Sam watches on, lost and alone as Bella looks up at Francesca, interpreting her words as she shouts, 'Where is Daddy going? Why is he in that police car?'

Francesca watches the car speed off down the street and disappear, the piercing whirling of the police sirens can hardly drown the children as they wail loudly. They repeatedly ask questions; Francesca needs answers too. She remains on the doorstep, bewildered and confused.

As the sound of the siren gradually fades, Francesca thinks of all the questions she needs to ask. *Who is Abigail West? Why is Sam involved in all of this? Murder! What evidence do they have? Is he guilty?* The mention of Olivia's name raises her suspicions. *Is that the reason he has been so distant from her recently?* Her thoughts and attention then change to focusing on Nico and Bella, she must be strong to protect them and keep them safe.

With her heart breaking she shuts the front door, turns around and crouches down to be at eye level with the kids, witnessing the fear in their eyes. She looks at Nico, kisses his cheek; looks at Bella, pushes her hair to the one side. It takes all her strength to remain calm and say, 'Kids, don't worry, everything will be OK. Dad is just going to talk with the police, and he will be back later, OK?' She tries her best to sound positive and convincing but inside she suspects she has just lost her best friend and husband of nine years. She draws her children closer, hugging them tightly. A tear rolls down her face, she dreams of home, back in Milan, surrounded, supported by her family and friends.

Over the past years, there have been many times when Francesca thought about relocating to Milan with the kids. In her mind, she visualises a beautiful image. The image of Nico and Bella eating gelato while walking around the city in the sunshine. For a long time, these dreams could only ever be exactly that, just a dream. Francesca has sacrificed so much of herself, her own joy and pleasure to be with Sam, to be there for him and help turn his dreams into a reality. As Francesca cradles her children, soothing them in the attempt to make them feel safe she wonders about what she wants, needs from life and for the first-time questions if staying in York with Sam is the right decision for the sake of the kids and her own happiness.

She thinks back to Sam's recent questionable behaviour and with this newfound information, it suggests that her once doting husband is now a stranger. A stranger hiding countless secrets from her.

Chapter 25

Friction. The handcuffs rub tightly against Sam's wrists, creating a deep burning sensation. As the police car speeds away, he notices the sadness on Francesca and the kids face. His family have never felt so far away from him. The car heads in the direction of North Yorkshire Police HQ. The two officers in the front of the car talk loudly over their radio, they are bombarded with updates on other cases and reports of petty crimes. The air in the back of the car feels stuffy and humid. Sam feels a tightness in his chest, his arms becoming numb as they are forced straight behind him. He is uncomfortable, both physically, and mentally. He wants nothing more than to escape and run in the direction of Olivia's house but realises this is not possible. This will never be possible. He closes his eyes and thinks about the forthcoming interrogation, how he should act, his manner and his answers. Sam knows the police will be watching, observing his every move, looking, assessing his non-verbal body language. *No sudden movements. Don't seem agitated. Just stay relax. Don't give the police a reason to suspect anything,* he reminds himself.

Sam opens his eyes to the sound of the intrusive clicking of the car indicator. He looks to see the Police HQ towering over the car, insecurities, and anxieties race into his consciousness, he is intimidated. Any remaining confidence is stripped away.

The car stops outside the entrance. DC Edwards opens the door and looks straight through Sam, without saying a word, he pulls onto the handcuffs and heads him in the direction of the entrance. Sam stumbles out of the car, looks up to the sky, breathes in the fresh air and walks with his head held high. DC Edwards directs Sam through reception into a small, windowless interrogation room. The room feels cold, lifeless with just a harsh glare beaming down from the fluorescent lighting. There is only a small table placed in between him and the detectives.

DC Clark and Edwards sit Sam down on a hard, wooden chair. DC Clark unlocks the handcuffs, Sam rubs his hands together, moving them around, easing the discomfort. His foot nervously taps the floor, he looks around the room, trying to remain calm and composed, noticing a tape recorder, notepad and pen on top of the table. There is a two-way window, the light from the fluorescent bars reflecting on the glass at the back of the room. Sam can't see through the glass but senses people behind it, there to closely observe him. He, forces a small, false smile towards the detectives, knowing he is being observed. The detective presses the tape record, a loud click can be heard as the interview begins.

DC Clark says, 'The day is Friday, June 10, 3:45 pm.' She continues by firstly advising Sam on his rights.

'What is your name?'

'Sam Johnson.'

'Mr. Johnson, what is your date of birth?'

'10 October 1986.'

'And what is your address?'

'Park Street, York.'

'Thank you. Do you know why you are here?'

The detectives start to question Sam on the alleged offences but he remains silent, showing no remorse or expression. The detectives sit back, waiting for Sam to answer but there is no response.

'OK, so we have evidence that links you to the death of Abigail West, ten years ago.'

Sam sits there, still, arms folded, a slight scowl flashes across his face.

DC Clark continues, 'We need to ask, what was your connection to her?'

There is no response.

'Is there anything you would like to say about that evening?'

Again, Sam continues to exercise his right to silence, the tension builds in the room.

'I want to explain to you that with new evidence this case will go to trial, with you as the prime suspect in Abigail's death.'

Sam finally answers, 'What, I don't understand?'

'Sam, this will be going to court so do you want to make a statement?'

Sam bemused, shakes his head. 'No, I would like to request a lawyer.'

'OK, that can be arranged. If you aren't happy to answer any questions around the Box Hill case, let's move on and talk about Olivia Bloom. You met her at New Dawn Architects. When we saw you two days ago, you mentioned the last time you saw her was Monday in the office, is this information still correct?'

Sam looks directly at DC Clark, he shakes his head slightly, as if to try and clear all the thoughts bouncing around his mind. 'Yes, Monday, correct.'

'Mr. Johnson we now have evidence that conflicts with that.'

DC Clark leans back into her chair, more confident.

'Let me ask you, again, what were you doing on Tuesday?'

Sam fidgets and looks down at the floor.

'Tuesday? I went to the office in the morning then left at lunch time to head to a meeting, was in town for a couple of hours then headed back home,' Sam states, a slight tone of arrogance in his voice.

'Where did you go after the meeting?'

'After the meeting?' There is a pause. 'I just said I went straight home.'

DC Clark raises her voice slightly. 'I want to repeat that this is your opportunity to give your account.' She repeats the question, 'Were you at home all afternoon and evening on Tuesday?'

Sam shuffles in his chair, trying to get comfortable. He is chewing the inside of this mouth, eyes widening, staring in the direction of the detectives. He finally responds, 'Yes. I didn't see Olivia that day.'

DC Clark leans forward on the table, her fingers interlocked making direct eye contact with Sam, 'You didn't see Olivia? Our statement contradicts that. We have a statement from Olivia that mentions an attack took place at her house in the afternoon. We have also found blood droplets in the lounge carpet and on a hand towel in the house. The forensics are sending over the sample to see if it matches your genetic markers.'

The officer pauses, notices Sam sinking into his sink, a look of anguish plastered across his face, 'And from what we have been told Mr. Johnson, we have a strong suspicion that it will.'

Sam folds his arms, leans back in his chair, and tilts his head to the side with a tense expression on his face.

'Sam, do you have anything to say?'

He looks down to the floor, unresponsive.

The lack of response is starting to frustrate the officers.

DC Clark leans in towards Sam, 'Sam, I am going to reason with you, it isn't looking good. The evidence is stacked up against you. We want to know what happened between you and Olivia. This is your time to give your account of events.'

Sam can't believe that there is now a witness in the Box Hill case, after all this time. He has been fearful of this for many years but assumed that, after ten years, the possibility of someone coming forward or there being new evidence is extremely remote.

A knock sounds on the interview room door. The police officers' glance at each other, ignore the interruption and continue questioning. The knock is repeated. The tape recorder is paused.

An irritated DC Clark shoots outs of her chair and directly asks the male officer who is standing outside the door, 'What is so urgent, we are in the middle of questioning a suspect.'

The male officer whispers something to DC Clark quietly enough that Sam can't hear what is being said. They talk for some minutes. *What is taking so long,* he wonders?

DC Clark closes the door and walks back over to the table, still standing, she says, 'Mr. Johnson, there is more information in the Olivia Bloom case. Do you know someone called Harry Akington?'

Sam responds, 'Yes, he is Olivia's ex of five years, why is that important?'

DC Clark answers, 'He has seen the missing persons article and has just given a statement. It seems he was with Olivia on Tuesday afternoon. When they met up, Olivia told him about the affair and stalking. Olivia has also confided in Harry about the pregnancy.'

'Pregnancy? What do you mean pregnant?' Sam immediately reacts.

Given Sam's reaction, it is apparent that he is oblivious to this information.

DC Clark continues, slightly confused, 'She is pregnant, Sam. Just so we are clear, did you not know that information?'

'No!' Sam shouts louder than he anticipated. 'What, whose baby is it?'

'From the statement we have just been given from Mr. Akington, we believe the baby is yours, Mr. Johnson.'

Sam pulls the chair back, crouches over and puts his head into his hands, he gently rocks back and forward. Not saying a word for a while, until he stutters into his palms, 'I just can't believe this, any of this.'

DC Edwards inquisitively asks, 'Given the fact that you are married and Miss. Bloom is pregnant with your child, is this what led to the altercation at her house on Tuesday?'

'No, the argument had nothing to do with the fact that she is pregnant, like I said, I didn't know.'

A small smile sweeps across the officer's face, 'So, you just admitted that an argument did take place at her house on Tuesday. If you didn't know about the baby, can you tell us what the argument was about then?'

Sam looking flustered, naively continues, 'Look it has been a long day, can I leave now, I am happy to chat through this tomorrow?'

'Mr. Johnson, I think I need to spell this out to you. You are being charged with the murder of Abigail West. We also now have the statement from Olivia Bloom. Forensics have been at Miss. Bloom's house; they have already sent off to the lab blood samples they have found. If the blood matches your genetic markers, you will then be charged with the separate case of aggravated assault against Miss. Bloom. As far as we are concerned, you are potentially a threat to society, so you will be detained in custody until trial, with no option for bail.'

Sam freezes in shock. DC Edwards walks around to him and puts the handcuffs on once again. Sam stands up, his wrists behind his back. He is taken through the police station to a small, dark, concrete cell. There are no windows, and any small amount of light that comes through is stolen sunlight from the central hallway. The confided space puts his senses into overdrive; the low temperature in the room makes Sam freeze. The darkness is overwhelming and the silence, deafening. Thoughts rush through his brain. He walks around the cell analysing the small veins and cracks that run through the walls. Sam stares at the pattern, the small details on the concrete to distract his mind and focus on something else that isn't the current reality. A reality where he has no freedom or power. He has never been great at relinquishing control, so being caged in a cell begins to play havoc on his mind.

Time passes. He hears heavy steps in the hallway, the noise is getting closer and louder. Are they coming to see Sam? Are they releasing him? No, nobody comes, he is there, alone, isolated, only his dark thoughts to keep him company.

Chapter 26

The trauma of watching someone you love been escorted away in a police car is too much to bear, Francesca thinks, agonises over what is going on. All she wants is to be alone, trying to make sense of her life that in one quick moment has shattered into a million fragmented pieces.

What she needs to soothe the pain is for Sam to walk back through the door, explain that there has been a misunderstanding and then give the whole family a warm, familiar embrace. But that never happens, instead the only communication between them is a short, abrupt phone call from the police station.

'Cesca, it's me!' Desperation echoing through his voice.

Francesca yells, 'What the fuck is going on, Sam?'

'Try to keep calm, my darling.'

'Keep calm? How is that possible when you have just been arrested after being charged with murder! You better start talking. What the hell is going on, Sam?'

'I don't know yet.'

'What do you mean you don't know?'

'It has all happened so quick, Cesca.'

'Who is this Abigail West and why are the police saying you are connected to her death?

Sam doesn't respond.

Francesca pleads for answers, 'And Olivia Bloom, the police said you assaulted her?'

'There is a lot I need to explain, I can't do that now.'

'So when? I presume you will be granted bail tomorrow, when you come home, you better start talking.'

Francesca listens intently for a response but there is nothing. She repeats the question, getting increasingly impatient, 'Tomorrow?'

'Cesca, I am not being granted bail.'

'I don't understand, why not?'

'Like I said, there is a lot I haven't told you. I maybe should have, but everything that happened with Abigail was in my past. My past. I never expected it to find a way to damage my future.'

'Your future? You mean our future as a family, or is that not even a consideration? I clearly don't know who you are. I mean what am I going to tell the kids?'

Sam's voice breaks slightly on the phone. 'Just say I am working some things out and will be back soon.'

'When exactly is soon then?' Francesca demands.

'As soon as the trial is over, I will hopefully be out and back at home, together with you all.'

Francesca's voice gets louder. 'You still haven't explained. Why are you on trial?'

'I can't discuss that, not right now.'

'If you can lie to me about something this big, what else have you been hiding from me?'

Sam doesn't respond, he thinks about whether he should mention everything else, Olivia, their affair and now the baby. Instead, he thinks about his own needs and right now he needs the support of his family. 'Nothing, I haven't lied about anything else. I promise you.'

Nico and Bella can be heard shouting in the distant.

'I have got to go and feed the kids dinner. I suppose we will speak soon.'

Before Sam can even answer, Francesca slams the phone down and the line rings dead.

Francesca had hoped the call with Sam would give some clarity on the situation. Instead, the call just made her realise that after all this time, her relationship with her husband and best friend has not been real. Total devastation at the realisation that their time together has been full of lies and deceit.

Her mind is confused, unclear as to what to think about all the unanswered questions that spiral out of control. But without Sam's presence, Francesca has the space to think about what she truly wants from life. Sam has always been a focal point of her life, her past, but now she is becoming unsure if he will feature a major part of her future.

Chapter 27

A tight cocoon, Lily is wrapped up in Charlie's arms, safe and content. She feels protected by his embrace and warmth, his heart beating through his chest onto her back. The pale bedroom curtains sway in the morning air. She lies wide awake, content in this grand feeling of love. She stays still, feeling grateful for this man who has helped her see that she does deserve to love and be loved. Charlie moves slightly in the bed gradually waking. Half asleep, he reaches over and kisses Lily gently on her cheek. Lily turns over, and they look at each other, face to face. No words need to be said, they both know how they feel, Charlie strokes the hair away from her face.

She thinks about the recent conversation with the police officer. Wanting to be open with Charlie, she starts to fidget restlessly. Sam, sensing there is something on Lily's mind asks, 'Everything alright?' This is her moment to reveal her past, be authentic and make him understand her old life. She can hear Mr. Lint saying, 'Vulnerability creates intimacy.' Lily isn't going to hide in the shadows of her past anymore.

Taking a deep breath, she begins to explain everything. With every word, she goes deeper, exploring and revealing details of her old life, life with her beautiful mum, then having to adjust to a life without her mum. How she won't be by her side when she achieves life milestones, falling in love, hopefully getting married and one day having children. Knowing her mum will never witness these joyous occasions is devastating, truly heart-breaking. Tears stream uncontrollably from Lily's eyes. Charlie sits silently, listening compassionately, which gives her the confidence to continue to break her walls down even further.

Lily describes her past unhelpful coping strategies, a near addiction with alcohol, the dark places she thought she would never come back from. Finally, she reaches the most difficult part, conscious that she may be judged. She confesses that she was a potential witness to a murder, how she had recently seen Sam Johnson in the news and how she gave a statement to the police.

She mentions that she will be going on record and testifying in court, wanting, needing him to be there, if he can be there, even if that does mean travelling from Australia to York. Asking this of him will confirm if their relationship is a holiday romance, or one based on more solid foundations.

Any concern Lily may have had about Charlie's response, disappears instantly when he moves closer to Lily, touching her face and says confidently, 'You have been through so much. I can't believe how difficult that must have been to tell me. I am proud of you, Lils, every day you surprise me with your strength and determination.'

Lily takes a moment to think over the recent revelations shared with Charlie, feeling as if a weight has been lifted from her shoulders.

Watching Lily feel more relaxed and confident, Sam continues, empathetically, 'You know this was never in my plan. I didn't expect to move to Australia and...' There is a long pause. Lily tries to anticipate the words that are about to follow. With his hands still on her face, he smiles and says to her, '...never expected to fall in love with someone.'

Lily exhales with relief, edges closer to Charlie, smiles and responds, 'Charlie, I love you too.'

Charlie whispers to Lily, 'You mean everything to me. I know this is important to you, let me know how I can help. I will of course be there for you, with whatever you need.'

Lily sinks down further into the sheets, becoming increasingly vulnerable, she says, nervously, 'The court case will be in a couple of months. When I leave, I will probably be back in England for about a month. I don't know if you have any time off, but if you do, I would love more than anything to have you there with me.'

'Of course, like I said, I am here for you. Don't worry about anything.'

Lily watches Charlie's mouth as he speaks, so confident and reassuring. She replies, 'I don't know what I would do without you. Depending on how long we have in England, we could make it into a holiday, see our family and friends. What do you think?'

Charlie strokes her face, running his fingers over her cheeks. 'That sounds like a great idea.'

She rests her head on Charlie's chest, closing her eyes. It has been a long time since she has felt so protected. For so long Lily has run away from herself, her thoughts that have been weighing her down, keeping her from truly living. As she imagines sitting in the stand watching Sam Johnson walk away in handcuffs, an overwhelming sense of relief and closure causes her eyes to well up. In that moment, Lily decides to book her flights and face her past. Without hesitation, she jumps out of bed, opens her phone and redials the last inbound call.

The international dial tone rings. There is an answer.

'Hello, DC Clark, it's Lily Hayes here, we spoke recently about the case against Sam Johnson. I am ready to go on record and give a full statement.'

'Lily, it is lovely to hear from you. That is great news. Mr. Johnson is currently detained in custody. I just want to reiterate that with your statement, this will now go to court. We will give you as much notice as we can, but I guess the trial will be in the next few months.'

Lily takes a deep breath, 'OK, I am ready. I suppose in a way I have been preparing myself for ten years to face up to this.'

Lily gives the statement and mentions every detail possible of that night. She talks through her senses, what she saw and heard during the party.

That was it, nothing more Lily can do now; she has to wait patiently for notification of the trial date. She tries to not focus on what this will entail but she is ready to step out of her comfort zone and seek closure.

Chapter 28

Olivia found the experience of delivering her statement to the Sussex Police emotionally draining, yet cathartic. Returning to her parent's house, she must now face the bombardment of missed calls from Robert. When she finally returns his calls, she explains everything, how everything changed the day she became emotionally involved with Sam. There are a couple of details she keeps to herself, including the pregnancy. Robert on hearing the news expresses regret for hiring Sam, feeling responsible for bringing all this trouble to her. Olivia senses this is incredibly difficult for Robert to understand and accept so reassures him that none of it is his fault and moves the conversation on to another topic, work.

'Dare I ask what is going on with the Isla Bourne development?' Olivia enquires, interested in what has happened in her absence.

'Not much, Olivia. Without my two key architects working on the project, it has naturally stalled.'

'What has been said to Isla then?'

Robert responds, 'We have informed her that there has been a situation, one which we can't discuss, and the architects will no longer be assigned to the project. She was confused, frustrated with the delay it will cause on the project timelines. I believe another firm has been hired to take over from where you both left off.'

'I am so sorry, Robert, you know how seriously I take my job. Working as an architect has always been such a strong part of who I am, and my identity. I really wish that I hadn't got caught up in all of this. More than anything I want to turn back time, a time before Sam. It was all so much easier then.'

Robert softens his tone even more. 'I bet. Look, take as much time off as you need and come back to us as soon as you are ready.'

'Thanks, Robert. I think it is probably best if I stay in Sussex for the moment. Being with my family is just what I need now.' Olivia sighs and continues, 'I do want to come back to work but not just yet.'

Robert replies compassionately, 'Whenever you are ready, we are here for you.'

After the unexpected events she takes the time to try and process the information, until some weeks later a call comes through from York Police advising that a trial date has been set for a separate case involving Mr. Johnson. The police inform that due to new recent evidence he is being charged with murder. The shocking news makes her shiver, truly devastated for the victim and her family.

Listening to the words, "*Charged with Murder*" makes Olivia question the person she was dating, did she even know the real Sam Johnson at all? She explains to the police that she would like to attend the trial, in the hope that it will shed some light on the character of the father of her child, a person she thought she once knew.

As time rolls on, Olivia with the help of her parents tries to regain her physical and mental strength. Before she knows it, she is booking her twelve-week scan with the hospital, back in York. As she leaves Sussex in preparation of this next chapter, she feels vulnerable without the shield of protection from her parents.

Arriving home after the altercation, she is acutely aware of the police and forensics investigators that have treated her home as a crime scene. As Olivia steps through the door, she is flooded by flashbacks of a past traumatic event, but she uses her strength to finds a sense of calm. Rubbing her small, growing stomach, she feels totally connected, knowing that there is now a baby to focus on. The next two months waiting for the trial is agonising, Olivia tries to resume normality being back at work, doctor appointments, seeing Harry and her close friends. It has been over three months since the attack, but Olivia will not allow herself to remain a victim and she is ready to attend the trial, she wants to look Sam in the eye and show him her strength and resilience.

When the day of the trial arrives, the impending questions create chaos in Olivia's mind. *Is Sam a murderer? Will the truth be uncovered after all these years? Will the victim's family find any closure after finally knowing what happened that night?*

As Olivia and her parents approach York and Selby County Court, Olivia puts her head down and closes her eyes, trying to visualise being somewhere else, anywhere else.

She instantly becomes on high alert as the car brakes outside the courtroom, heart racing, palms sweaty, she is preparing to face Sam for the first time since the assault.

As she steps out of the car, in the distance there is a tall silhouette of a man with a big, bright smile, who is radiating warmth and kindness. Olivia looks in his direction and instantly feels at peace. It is Harry, he has turned up to support her. Seeing him there instantly makes her feel more at ease.

Olivia walks over to him slowly, speechless at his selfless and caring nature. He never mentioned that he would attend.

Olivia with a warm, inviting smile says, 'Hello you.'

Her face relaxes, she quietly whispers, 'I didn't know you were coming here.'

'I wanted to. I couldn't bear to think about you going through this, alone.'

Olivia wraps her arms around Harry in an intimate embrace, nestling her head into his shoulders. 'Well, I am not totally alone, mum and dad are here too. I really do appreciate this more than you will ever know.'

She closes her eyes; the outside world seems to fade away as she smells his familiar scent. It is only then that she realises how much she needs him to be there, with her.

'Thank you, Harry, for everything; I don't know what I would do without you.'

'Of course.'

She smiles, and gently rubs her stomach. Harry admires the visible changes to Olivia's body, 'You look beautiful, well you always are, pregnancy really does suit you.'

Too lost in conversation, they fail to notice Olivia's parents who are now standing behind them.

Her dad interrupts the conversation. 'Harry, good to see you. It is so nice of you to be here and support our Liv in this.'

'Mr. Bloom, good to see you, it has been a while! How are you?'

'Good thanks, we will all be better when this is over' her dad says, referring to the court case. The two men start to walk inside.

Olivia's mum interlocks their arms and whispers, 'You know, I always liked him.'

Olivia smiles to herself, 'I know you do. After all this time, I do too, maybe more than I thought.'

Right then and there she forgets where she is, feeling content, surrounded by people that she loves, and has always loved.

Chapter 29

The last couple of months have been disruptive for Lily, Francesca and Olivia, with the same common factor, Sam Johnson. These three women may be strangers, but they are connected and the trial will be the first time they will be together in the same room. The day is finally here when Sam will face a judge and jury, as well as Abigail West's family, to discuss his version of the events that night at the party.

The courtroom begins to fill with people taking a seat on wooden benches. The subtle sounds of people whispering vibrate through the room. Everyone anxiously anticipates the beginning of the trial.

Lily enters the court, scans her environment then takes her designated place on the front bench, ready to be cross-examined by Sam's lawyers. Charlie follows her lead and sits a couple of rows behind her. Olivia walks into the courtroom, her support system acting as her armour, giving a layer of protection. By contrast, Francesca arrives alone; she looks nervously around the room to see unfamiliar faces each with a companion, someone they love by their side. Witnessing this reinforces the feeling that, away from her family and friends in Milan, in a new city, she is all alone.

Olivia looks around the room trying to see if Sam's wife will be in attendance. She remembers what she looks like from the background photo on Sam's phone, an image portraying much happier times. Given her affair with Sam, a deep sensation of guilt floods Olivia's body. She wonders if the Johnson family will ever be the same again. She sees the side profile of a beautiful Italian woman with short, black hair. Over the last couple of nights, Olivia has agonised about coming face to face with Francesca and what she would say, if anything at all. She believes now that Francesca deserves to know the truth. Olivia has made the decision to tell her everything about the affair with Sam.

Suddenly, anticipation in the court heightens as people shuffle on their seats ready to get a first glimpse of the jury that are now walking in. The jury panel are a mixture of sexes and ages. As they take their places, eyes then divert to the judge who walks confidently into the court. The next arrival will be Sam Johnson who will walk into the room to have his fate decided.

As the defendant enters, all eyes focus sharply on him, judging him. A man who once carried himself with confidence is now sheepishly looking down at the ground. His light brown hair is unusually dishevelled. He is being led by a police officer who is holding onto his handcuffs. As they are removed, he takes a seat in the dock for the accused. Sam looks a shadow of the person he once was. There is a haunted expression across his face.

The judge makes her opening remarks to the jury as to their rules of conduct and cautions that they should only find the defendant guilty if it is beyond reasonable doubt that he did commit murder. She then asks the Prosecuting QC to give the opening statement.

The confident QC walks over to the jury walking up and down the stand, making eye contact with every member of the panel using careful and precise words as she makes her opening statement.

'Good morning, my name is Ms Williams, I am the lead counsel in the case of Regina v Sam Johnson. It is my task to lay the facts of this case before you and to prove that on the 12 May 2012, the defendant Mr. Sam Johnson committed the worst possible of crimes, murder; a sexually motivated murder where he exerted force over a 19-year-old girl, Abigail West. Members of the jury, we will call a key eyewitness who was at the party where Miss. West was murdered and saw this brutal attack take place. At the conclusion of the case, and after you have heard all the evidence, we are confident that you will return a verdict, charging Sam Johnson, Guilty of Murder.'

It is then immediately followed by Sam's defence lawyer who makes his opening statement.

'Good morning, your honour, members of the jury. My name is Jason Park, representing the defendant, Sam Johnson. Your honour, my client attended a friend's party in Box Hill, ten years ago, where he met Miss. West on the evening of the 12 May 2012. During the evening they connected. There is no denying that Mr. Johnson and Miss. West engaged in sexual intercourse and I would like to clarify that the sex was consensual between both parties. After Miss. West's death, Mr. Johnson gave a statement to the police but there was not enough evidence to connect him to this crime. This case is brought upon the court today as Miss. Lily Hayes has recently come forward as a witness. Miss. Hayes is now testifying after a long period of ten years to suggest that Mr. Johnson murdered Abigail West. I will demonstrate that Mr. Johnson is a family man, happily married with two young children. He is an award-winning Architect with a successful career and is not a criminal. I am sure that, when you have carefully heard and considered all the facts, you will come to the only logical verdict, that of Not Guilty. Thank you.'

Lily looks towards the jury as her name is announced in the opening statement, a feeling of dread arising. Her legs start to tremble, beginning to feel overwhelmed. She takes deep breaths and looks behind to see the presence of Charlie, reassuring her. Suddenly her name is called, she stands up and walks past the defendant, legs feeling weightless, almost unable to carry her. Lily reaches the witness stand, looking out to a sea of unknown faces, and fixes her eyes on the one face she wishes she would never have to see again. She is ready to tell her account and relive the night, all over again, this time, hopefully for the last time.

Lily takes the judge and jury through every detail of that night, her encounter, her intuition, what she saw and heard. Mr. Park cross-examines and scrutinises her every word, trying to break down and find holes in her story, asking why after ten years she is only coming forward now and how certain can she be of what she saw, given the fact she was under the influence at the time.

She explains, with a heartfelt tone about her life journey, losing her mum and feeling so isolated that she resorted to alcohol, and on that night, for the first and only time, drugs. Lily advises that even though she didn't know the intention of Sam's action, she is certain of what she saw and wouldn't have testified if there was any doubt in her mind. That even after ten years, when she saw his name in the paper in relation to a Missing Persons case, she knew the importance of ringing the police to tell them everything.

It is clear from the defence lawyer's questioning that the outcome of the verdict relies heavily on Lily's testimony. Lily has given her version of events, that's all she can do. She sits back in the stand, feeling relieved that she has done the right thing. It is now time for Sam to be cross examined.

Sam has never previously spoken about that night with Abigail. He has pushed all thoughts of regret and remorse out of his mind. As he is called to the stand to explain his side of the story, in front of everyone he can no longer avoid the event. Sitting opposite all these faces that are glaring at him, he feels incredibly exposed. He searches the crowd, looking for the two faces he must see, Francesca and Olivia. He knows there is no repairing his relationship with Olivia but what about Francesca? He thinks about whether she will forgive him when she finds out the darkness hidden in his past?

Reminding himself of the enormity of his responses, he takes a second to block out everyone and everything in the room and composes himself, trying to give off the impression of being calm and collected.

'Mr. Johnson, during the evening of 12 May 2012, what was happening at the party before your encounter with Miss West?'

'Everyone was having a good time, drinks were flowing, the house was full of people, like any other party, I suppose.'

'Were you just drinking?'

'Yes.'

'And were any other substances consumed?'

'Substances? Like what?'

'Marijuana, cocaine?'

'No, I don't do drugs. I was just drinking a mixture of tequila, whisky, and beer.'

'The results of Miss. West's post-mortem showed a high level of cocaine in her system. Are you saying that she took drugs, but you didn't?'

'That's correct.'

'When did you first meet Miss. West?'

'At the party, that night. We were introduced by mutual friends who thought we would get on.'

'So, you met that night for the first time? Can you fill in the blanks between what happened from when you first met Miss. West to her being found dead early the following morning, on the 13 May in an upstairs bedroom?'

'After we were introduced, we drank some tequila. She mentioned she wanted to travel and go to university, just standard conversation really.'

'Were you aware that Miss. West had been taking drugs?'

'No.'

'How did she seem when you were having this discussion?'

'Fine, happy, we were enjoying each other's company.'

'So, you are talking, getting on well. Miss. Hayes reports that she saw you both together in the upstairs bedroom, so how did your actions lead you there?'

'We had been talking for a while in the lounge. It was loud, full of people shouting and music blaring. We were sitting on the sofa, and then suddenly, she leans over and kisses me. I was attracted to her, so I responded. She then asked if I wanted to go somewhere quieter. I stood up, took her hand and walked into the hallway, up the grand staircase and found an empty bedroom at the end of a long corridor.'

'What time did you head upstairs?'

'It was late in the evening. Around 11:30 pm I guess.'

'You are suggesting that Miss. West instigated the opportunity to have sexual relations with you and that she was a willing participant?'

'Yes. There was definite sexual chemistry between us.'

'So, you both go to the bedroom, then what?'

'We closed the door slightly and started kissing. It was intense.'

The lawyer doesn't say anything, he allows Sam to take the lead.

Sam continues, 'After a while, we got undressed and started to have sex. We were both having a good time.'

'How do you know that for sure?'

Sam begins to shift around his chair, looking uncomfortable as he discloses the information in front of his wife and a room of strangers. 'Well, she was kissing me, making noises.'

'Mr. Johnson if I can stop you there. When Lily Hayes gave her statement, she found the noises were a key factor in knowing that something uncomfortable was happening in the bedroom. The bedroom that you and Miss. West were in. Can you elaborate for me as to why Miss. Hayes would say that?'

Sam pauses then responds, 'Well, I suppose the noise from Abigail was moaning. Moaning from excitement and pleasure.'

The lawyer continues to press further, talking slowly and clearly, 'In the evidence just given by Miss. Hayes, she states that the sounds were loud, dominating and piercing. Mr. Johnson that does not indicate a woman enjoying herself?'

Sam presses his lips together. He takes a moment to glance back into the audience, and his eyes make contact with Francesca. When Sam sees her, she is looking down at the floor, shaking her head, obviously uncomfortable.

Given the delay in Sam response to the question, the lawyer repeats, 'Would you now agree with Miss. Hayes's version of the event?'

Sam demands, 'No, I wouldn't!'

'Mr. Johnson, the noises in that room made Miss. Hayes uncomfortable that she had to investigate further what was happening.'

There is still no response from Sam, the prosecution pushes on.

'Also, in her statement Miss. Hayes said that she saw you with your hands around Miss. West's neck. Can you explain that?'

'It was part of the experience. She was into it.'

'How do you know that? Did she say so?'

'No, I can just tell.'

'So, she didn't consent, and you continued to essentially strangle Miss. West?'

The tension between them to starts to build, Sam's heart beats, he feels uneasy and begins to lose patience with the line of questioning and says, 'I wasn't strangling her.'

'The witness states she saw you putting increasing pressure on her neck.'

Sam states louder, 'I wasn't!'

'Mr. Johnson, Miss. West's post-mortem showed that she died of asphyxiation, and we now have a witness who claims to have seen your hands around Miss. West's neck. That is rather a coincidence, would you not agree? You have already explained that you were drinking heavily, is it not fair to say that your view on what happened could be somewhat distorted?'

Sam fidgets in his seat, getting irritable and frustrated, 'I suppose so.'

'Miss. West's death was the result of persistent pressure on her neck.' The lawyer pauses, walks up and down, passing by the jury stand before she turns back to face Sam. Her voice rises in a more dominating manner. 'There are national reports that indicate a significant rise in the number of women dying through being choked during sex.'

The lawyer pauses, walks back over so she is now opposite Sam, who remains motionless. Their only communication is eye contact. The court is silent, still, assessing Sam and his answers, wondering what may now follow.

'You were told when you were a suspect ten years ago that your DNA was all over Miss. West. You admitted then and now to having sex with her. But what I still do not understand is why Abigail was found in the bedroom that you were in together, dead?'

The lawyer senses Sam's frustration and pushes on. 'Mr. Johnson, could your encounter with Miss. West have been a case of a sexual game gone wrong?'

Sam's demeanour instantly changes; he drops his head to look down at the ground, shakes his head, side to side. As he does so, the members of the audience and jury move forward slightly on their bench as if this will enhance their hearing of what will be said next.

'Your reckless behaviour and disregard for this innocent woman resulted in her death.'

Sam remains silent.

'I am going to need a response from you.'

Time passes slowly until Sam mutters quietly, 'I…' He pauses again, head still looking downwards, uncomfortably moving around his chair. He shakes his light brown hair as if wanting his hair to hide his face from the world.

After a long pause he then shouts, disorientated, 'I didn't mean to kill her!'

An intense sound of gasps and people murmuring reverberates around the courtroom, quietly at first then grows louder and louder. So disruptive, the judge asks for order to quieten the court down.

Sam shocked at the confession that has just come out of his mouth, tries again. 'I mean it was an accident, it went too far. Please know it was never my intention.'

There is a long pause.

'Mr. Johnson, so you have admitted to murdering Miss. West, ten years ago. Can I ask why you didn't come forward at the time and tell the truth?'

Sam pushes his chair back in the stand, crouches over and rests his elbows on his knees. He looks down to the floor, the people in the court looking at the top of his head.

He remains silent, the lawyer becomes impatient so presses on, 'Mr. Johnson, do I need to ask you again?'

Before she has time to finish her statement, Sam blurts out interrupting her, 'I didn't know what to do. I knew it was wrong, I felt guilty and wanted to run away from the situation.'

All eyes fixate on Sam.

He shakes his head, eyes vacant, 'I have been running away from that night and the truth for a decade now. Now the truth is out there, I no longer have to continue living a lie.'

He raises his head slightly, tilts to the side and looks over to the jury, and for one final plea says, 'I am sorry, the guilt of this has imprisoned me for far too long. I never meant for it to happen.'

The lawyer turns to the judge and says, 'That's all, your honour.' For the first time in ten years the truth has finally been uncovered.

Chapter 30

The court takes a quick break. The audience spill out of the courtroom, excitement and nervous energy is palpable as people talk about the case and the latest revelation.

It is a couple of hours before the usher mentions the case will be resuming. The courtroom refills with people eager to know the outcome. Sam sits silently, facing the judge, his hands held together on top of the table, his left foot tapping the floor in terrifying anticipation of the verdict.

The feeling in the room is heavy and tense.

The jury is positioned to the side of the court, the foreman, a middle-aged man, stands up, holds out a piece of paper and addresses the court. Sam takes in the grandeur of the room, the tall high ceilings and imagines all the people in the courtroom gazing towards him waiting to see how he will react to the verdict.

The statement is read out:

'On the count of murder, we find the defendant "*Not Guilty*".'

Sam exhales a large sigh of relief.

The foreman continues, 'On the count of manslaughter, we find the defendant…Guilty.'

Sam's eyes glaze over as two police officers walk towards him, holding out handcuffs.

Silent whispers and conversations immediately circulate in the courtroom.

The judge turns her attention to the courtroom and begins her statement, 'I would like to take this time to acknowledge the death and loss of Miss. West. My thoughts are with the family. And Mr. Johnson, this irresponsible, reckless act resulted in the death of a young and innocent woman. I appreciate this was not your intention, but I do need to take into consideration the loss of life. In addition, there is the fact that you should have made your statement ten years ago. My primary objective here is to protect society. I will give serious consideration to the circumstances and the verdict which has been passed and will issue the sentence at a later date. However, make no mistake, the sentence will be one of a prison term.'

The finality of the words spoken sends an electric shock through Sam's body. Prison. The information becomes difficult for him to process. He feels numb as he stands up, his back now to the court, not wanting to be seen by Francesca or Olivia, or even face the reality of what is about to happen. The shame of the situation is too much to bear. The handcuffs pinch his wrists as he is escorted out of the courtroom.

Suddenly, just as he is about to leave the courtroom, he takes a quick moment to turn and face Francesca, who is storming out of court. He then focuses his attention on Olivia; she is standing there, tall, and confident, looking directly at him with a look of disgust on her face. Sam notices her demeanour and then her growing bump. In total shock and heartbreak, he opens his mouth, as if to say something but he knows now there is nothing he can say. The effect of his obsessive and impulsive nature has jeopardised both his future and freedom. All he can do is turn his back on the two women he loves and has now, lost.

Chapter 31

Francesca, Lily and Olivia watch on as justice has now been served. Francesca can't believe what has just unfolded in court. How can she respond to all of this? There is no appropriate outlet in the courtroom for her to express the anger and rage permeating her every cell. How could her husband, the father of their children, have killed this woman? She has never felt more alone.

As Sam is escorted away, she can't even look in his direction, instead a wave of confusion floods over her. With Sam now being sent to prison, the life she once knew has been destroyed.

She needs to rebuild her life and start putting her own happiness, Nico and Bella first. Her children need role models to look up to and admire, and with no support system in York her mind switches again to Milan and what her life with her children could be like if they did relocate there.

Lily, upon hearing Sam's confession, feels sheer relief. She realises there can now be closure to the burden of guilt she has carried heavy on her shoulders. It has been a long and daunting journey for her. Right now, in this moment she is proud of her decision. She has immense pride and confidence of what she has achieved in the past six months, meeting Mr.

Lint, giving her statement and finding love with Charlie, this is her time to move forward and enjoy life, a life that is not filled with concerns and regrets. Lily is safe and at peace, finally after all this time, she has found a sense of redemption.

Olivia cannot quite believe the news. The man she knew to be charismatic and successful has killed a woman. She feels great sadness for Abigail, her family and the torment they must have been through. Her memory flashes back over her tumultuous relationship with Sam, seeing his temper, anger and the increasing desire for control in their sexual encounters. She rests her head on Harry's shoulder and allows tears to stream from her eyes. There is also a strong element of feeling lucky that she has escaped his wrath. In such close proximity to Francesca, she wonders, once again, if the right thing to do is approach her and tell her even more of Sam's hidden secrets.

Outside the courtroom door, crowds of people have gathered, they are all talking about the case. Olivia searches for Francesca wanting to catch her eye amongst the sea of people. Then through a small gap she sees her. Olivia turns to face Harry and says, 'Will you wait here? There is something I have to do before we go.'

Olivia moves through the crowd of people, keeping her eyes fixed on Francesca. As she approaches her, she takes a deep breath and smiles gently before saying, 'Hi, hello.'

A confused Francesca responds quizzically, 'Hello. Do I know you?'

'No, you don't. I used to work with your husband. My name is Olivia Bloom.' Francesca last heard the name, Olivia Bloom when Sam was arrested at their house.

'Yes, I heard your name when my husband was arrested at our home. There was a mention of an alleged assault?' There is a short pause before Francesca continues, 'So can I ask, did he assault you?'

'Yes, he did, I made a statement, and I will be pressing charges.'

A tired and frustrated Francesca responds, 'OK. Look as you can imagine it has been a long day, is that what you came over to tell me?'

Olivia face saddens, 'Sadly not. There is more.'

Francesca frowns as Olivia continues talking.

'There is no easy way for me to tell you this, but I think you have a right to know.' As Olivia speaks, she looks down to her growing belly and places a soothing hand on her stomach.

'OK, what is it then?'

The sound of people bustling past the women only heightens the surrounding tension in the air.

'Sam and I were working on a project together, and after a while we got close. Too close. We knew it was wrong, so wrong, but we started having an affair, it lasted a month, or so. At the time I wasn't thinking clearly.'

Francesca's face tightens, 'Everything is starting to make sense, we came to York and soon after we moved here he became so distant, now I presume it was because of this?' A disheartened Francesca repeats what she is being told, trying desperately to understand, 'An affair?'
Olivia nods slightly.

Francesca needs to know the full truth, as if it will help in her healing process, 'Ok, so what happened then, I mean between you?'

'After a while he started to get possessive there were a number of other events that happened, so I called it off. It's a long story but I suppose that's probably not important now.'

'After today and now hearing all this, sadly that doesn't seem to surprise me.' Francesca continues with a genuine tone and says, 'I am sorry about what has happened to you. Can I ask, why are you telling me all of this?'

Olivia creates a small, warm smile, 'Because I thought you have a right to know, I wanted to give you the full picture about what has been going on.'

A gentle sadness washes over Francesca's face. She makes a small frown, 'I don't know what to say. Ever since his arrest four months ago, I can't stop thinking about how I really don't know my husband at all. Maybe I never did.'

Olivia empathetically says, 'I am sorry, I truly am. You don't deserve this, any of this.'

'It has been a nightmare, really. A roller coaster not just for me, but for our kids as well, they don't deserve this.'

'There is one other thing I wanted to tell you.'

A confused Francesca looks on, *what else could there possibly be,* she thinks.

'I am pregnant.' Olivia looks down at her bump, her eyes are heavy, with a heartfelt tone she says, 'Francesca, the baby is Sam's.'

Francesca's jaw drops open, in total disbelief she sighs deeply and eventually she replies, 'When Sam was arrested, my heart broke into a million pieces. Before coming to court, I grieved for the loss of our relationship and what I naively thought was love. True love. It breaks my heart all over again to hear this news. Now, I know that our relationship was based on lies and deceit.'

Olivia's intuition takes over and she gently reaches out in support to hold Francesca's hands as she continues to talk.

'In a way, knowing the truth has opened my eyes for the first time in years. I can think about me and what is best for the kids. And what is best for our new family is to move back to Italy. I am desperately in need of that feeling of home, a place where we can feel safe and supported.'

Francesca holds onto Olivia's hands gently and continues, 'Thank you for telling me, it couldn't have been easy to approach me and tell me all of this but I am grateful that you did.'

The women exchange a warm smile.

Francesca looks down at Olivia's stomach and in a genuine, caring manner says, 'And good luck, with everything.'

Just for a fleeting moment, the women embrace.